TRICK OR TRAP

8

GOOSEBUMPS®
Also available as ebooks

ALSO AVAILABLE:

Goosebumps®

MOST WANTED

SPECIAL EDITION

TRICK OR TRAP

R.L. STINE

SCHOLASTIC INC.

Goosebumps book series created by Parachute Press, Inc.
Copyright © 2015 by Scholastic Inc.

All rights reserved. Published by Scholastic Inc., *Publishers since 1920.* SCHOLASTIC, GOOSEBUMPS, GOOSEBUMPS HORRORLAND, and associated logos are trademarks and/or registered trademarks of Scholastic Inc.

ISBN 978-0-545-62778-8

12 11   18 19

Printed in the U.S.A.   40
First printing 2015

PART ONE

1

My name is Scott Harmon. I'm twelve. Old enough not to be afraid of graveyards. Or creepy, old abandoned houses. Or scratchy creaking sounds late at night. Or howls or whispers or screeches or shadows darting in front of me, or loud car horns or bursts of cold wind or . . . or . . .

You probably get it. I'm old enough not to be afraid of a lot of things. But I still am. I mean, a lot of things make my heart skip a beat. Or make me choke or start to jump out of my skin. Or make me open my mouth in a *yelp* or a *hey* or a *heeelp*!

Sure, I tell myself to man up, to get braver. Do you think I don't wake up every morning and tell myself, "Scott, old buddy, old wimp, old fraidy-cat, today's the day you're not going to be scared of stuff!"?

I say that every morning. Then I push back the covers, lower my feet to the floor — and something happens. Maybe I step into a big bowl of ice water my evil sister, Rita, put beside the bed. And I start off the day with a loud, shrill scream.

Or maybe Rita slips some kind of animal under my sheets. Or maybe she leaves a frightening surprise, some creature big and ugly and dead, for me in my sock drawer.

Rita is bad. She is nine and very cute with big, round black eyes and dimples when she smiles. What makes her smile? Scaring me, her older brother, and watching me scream my head off.

She loves to frighten me and she's very good at it. Mom and Dad think she's adorable. I think she's a terror. And I mean *terror* in the horror-movie kind of way. Rita can be *terrifying*.

She even has an evil maniac laugh. If you heard it, you'd get chills, too. Seriously.

And let's face facts, Rita isn't my only problem.

As soon as I leave home, I've got Mickey Klass and his twin brother, Morty, in my face. The Klass brothers are like cavemen or Neanderthals. I mean, ape-men, primitive creatures you see in those science documentaries they make you watch in school.

They are only twelve, but they are very hairy. They both have stringy, long brown hair hanging down their chubby faces. I think they could grow beards if they wanted to. No joke. They're big and wide, built low to the ground, about the

4

same size as those Fiat cars you see on the street, maybe a little bigger.

And guess what? Their main mission in life is to terrify a kid we know and love named Scott Harmon.

When some people find out you're the kind of kid who is scared of things, they love to test you. They love to go after you. They love to make you squirm and scream and run.

Face it. They're *mean*. The Klass brothers are mean. It's like they saw the word *victim* tattooed on my forehead. Do you know that word?

Well, look it up. It will help explain why Mickey and Morty decided their new hobby would be scaring the pants off me and making my life miserable.

So you can see why I'm eager to change my whole personality. Maybe slip out of this skinny, quivering Scott Harmon body and into a powerful, muscle-bound X-Men body, afraid of nothing, bursting with mutant powers to zap anyone who challenges me.

I like Wolverine a lot. And sometimes I picture myself as Thor. He's big and quiet. He doesn't fit in, but he doesn't care. He doesn't take nonsense from anyone.

Sweet.

If only there were *brave* pills you could take. I'd gobble one every morning, go downstairs, and say, "Okay, Rita — do your worst." Or maybe on the walk to school: "Okay, Mickey and Morty — show me what you got!"

Can you imagine that?

Well, there aren't any brave pills. And the chances are not too good that I am actually a Marvel superhero in disguise.

That's why I have to say, "Hooray for Amanda Gold!" Amanda is my best friend, my pal. And she is as cowardly and wimpy and afraid of stuff as I am.

I'm not making this up. Ask her. She'll admit it.

When a mouse jumped across her desk last week in Ms. Mueller's class, Amanda screamed so loud, she set off all the fire alarms in the school. Why the fire alarms? I don't know. But you have to admit that's pretty awesome screaming.

After school, I told her how awesome that was. I mean, friends have to stick up for friends, right?

And now you are probably wondering why Amanda and I are out on this cold, blustery gray October afternoon. Across the street from the ancient graveyard. Huddled together, shivering, gazing up at the cracked and rickety front stoop of the dark, abandoned house everyone says is haunted.

Why are we here? That's what you're wondering, aren't you?

So am I.

2

Actually, I knew why we were here. I knew it but I didn't really believe it.

This was step one. The first part of our plan to make ourselves braver.

Halloween was coming soon. We had to toughen ourselves up. We had to be prepared.

Amanda and I talked about it for days. If we made ourselves tougher and less afraid, we could change our lives. And we could get what every frightened, timid person in the world wants. You guessed it.

Revenge.

First, I wanted to get revenge against my darling little sister, Rita.

This morning, Rita went into the bathroom before I woke up, emptied my mouthwash bottle, and filled it with some kind of red food coloring.

I know, I know. Most kids don't use mouthwash in the morning. But I have a thing about mouth germs. Don't judge me.

7

I was half-awake. I took a mouthful of the stuff and swished it around my mouth. Yuck. It tasted weird. I gazed in the mirror. I had RED TEETH! Red gums. *Blood all over my mouth. Blood!*

Did I scream in panic? Of course. You would, too, if you thought your mouth was dripping blood.

I could hear Rita laughing all the way from the kitchen downstairs.

So, yes, number one on my list is revenge against Rita.

And, of course, Amanda and I were eager to get revenge on Mickey and Morty. We weren't just eager, we were desperate to pay them back.

Did I mention their hobby is torturing Amanda, too?

So here we were, ready to prove to each other that we could change. We could become brave people in time for Halloween.

I was wearing a wool cap pulled down over my ears, my winter parka, and a woolly sweater underneath it. But I was still shivering. Amanda had her hands tucked deep in the pockets of her coat. A long blue scarf, wrapped round and around her, covered her mouth and nose.

The air was cold, and gusts of wind kept pushing against us, as if telling us to turn around and go home.

The sky was almost as dark as night. In the old graveyard behind us, the trees cracked and creaked in the wind.

Did I mention that the graveyard is just one block from where Amanda and I live? And that Lucky Me has to walk past it every morning and every afternoon to and from school?

Of course, I'm terrified of graveyards, and this one is particularly frightening. The gravestones are old, mostly rubbed smooth, cracked and tilted in every direction. It looks to me like the dead people have pushed up from under the ground, knocked over their tombstones as they pulled themselves up from their graves.

That's my worst nightmare. Well . . . *one* of them. That I'll be walking past the graveyard, and I'll see bony hands clawing the ground, someone slapping at the carpet of dead leaves from underground. A dead person . . . a *zombie* — pulling himself up from the cold, hard dirt. And then come staggering blindly toward me.

That's a bad nightmare, right? Don't snicker or laugh. If you lived one block from a graveyard, you might have that nightmare, too.

I pulled the collar of my coat higher. "Amanda, are we really doing this? Is this really going to make us braver? Are we making a big mistake?"

"Shut up," she said. "Stop talking."

"But —"

"We've already decided," she said, crossing her coat sleeves in front of her. "So shut up. And let's go."

9

I nodded. She was right. She knew me. She knew the Scott Harmon method for staying out of trouble. Just talk about doing something forever but don't really do it.

But like I said, we were desperate. We had to prove that we could be brave. We were going into the old, abandoned house. We had planned it, and now we were doing it.

Amanda took the first step onto the stoop and I followed. The stairs were made of some kind of gray stone, but they were cracked and crumbling.

No one had lived in this old house for a long, long time. Except maybe the ghosts. Everyone said the place was haunted. Everyone said weird howls and shrill cries rose from the house late at night.

I don't believe in ghosts. I mean, I don't *want* to believe in ghosts. So I sure hoped I wasn't going to run into any.

Amanda and I climbed the three steps of the front stoop. The front door was black, the paint peeling. I didn't see a doorbell. I mean, I didn't plan to ring the bell. I just didn't see one. The house was so old, maybe doorbells weren't invented then.

"Did you bring your phone?" Amanda asked. Her voice suddenly sounded tiny. Or was it just muffled by the swirling wind?

I tapped my jeans pocket. "Of course," I said. "I have it."

The plan, you see, was to sneak into the house, explore some rooms, and take pictures of us standing in there. The pictures would prove to the others that we were brave enough to go inside.

Amanda tilted her head toward the doorknob. "Try the door," she said.

"Why don't *you*?" I said.

"Oh, wow. Nice start," she snapped. "Totally brave, Scott. I'm impressed."

"If you're going to be sarcastic, we can do this some other time," I said.

She just stared at me with her cold blue eyes. I knew that stare. It meant *don't mess with me.*

I wrapped my hand around the pitted brass knob. Twisted it one way, then the other. I tried pulling the door open. Then I tried pushing.

And then I heard the raspy shout, a deep, angry, bellowing cry: *"Go away! Go away from my house!"*

"Huh?" My heart jumped to my throat, my knees folded, and I nearly fell off the stoop.

Amanda and I leaped back. We both spun away from the door. And I saw Mickey and Morty Klass grinning up at us from the sidewalk.

Mickey shook his head. "Scotty, you really thought that was a ghost — didn't you!"

He and his brother let out high-pitched giggles and bumped their hairy knuckles.

Their big, wide bodies were blocking the stoop. They wore furry brown coats that made them look like grizzly bears. Mickey's face was half-covered by a cap with furry brown earflaps. Morty wore the red-and-black baseball cap with a skull on the front that he always wears.

"Good joke, Mickey," I said. "Very funny."

"I'll tell you what's funny," Morty said. "Your faces!" The two of them laughed their cruel giggle again.

"Can we go now?" Amanda said.

"We just got here," Mickey said, adjusting his furry earflaps. "You don't want to hurt our feelings." He squinted his piggy eyes at Amanda. "What were you two doing? Trying to break into the house?"

"Bet they wanted to hide in there so they could kiss," Morty said. He made gross kissing sounds on the back of his hand.

They both howled with laughter.

Amanda scowled at them. "We were just looking around," she said. "Exploring."

"We have to go," I said. "Catch you guys later. I have to be home for my origami lesson."

Feeble. I know it. That was totally lame. But my brain just doesn't work well when these two hulks are breathing down my neck.

"I could do some origami on *you*," Mickey said. "Fold you up into a little bird."

"No thanks," I said. "My body doesn't fold. Really."

Morty reached up and poked my chest hard with two fingers. "Bet *we* could fold you," he growled. "Make you into a cute little bird and you could *cheep cheep cheep* like a canary."

"No thanks. I'm allergic to birds," I said. "I break out in big red bumps."

I gazed around, searching for an escape route. They had us trapped at the top of the stoop.

"Forget all that," Mickey said. "Scott and Amanda like to explore. So let's do some exploring."

"Yeah," Morty said. "We got a good place for you to explore. Let's go."

I didn't like the sound of this.

They grabbed us and pulled us off the stoop.

"Get your paws off me. Let us go," Amanda said. "Come on, guys. It's cold out here. Let us go."

They pushed us across the street to the low brick wall that runs around the graveyard. On the other side of the wall, the wind howled through the bare trees and sent clumps of dead leaves dancing over the gravestones.

"I really have to get home," I insisted. "I promised my little sister I'd show her how Velcro works."

The Klass brothers ignored me. They were grunting excitedly. They really did look like short, wide bears.

Amanda suddenly went pale. She crossed her arms tightly in front of her. I saw her shiver. "We're in trouble," she whispered.

"Good thing you like to explore," Mickey said, unable to keep an evil grin from spreading across his face. "Since you two lucky dudes just joined the Dare Club."

I swallowed. "Dare Club? What's *that*?" My voice cracked.

Mickey's grin didn't fade. "We dare you to do things, and you do them."

Amanda hugged herself. "What if we don't want to join?"

The two hulks burst out laughing. "You're already lifetime members!" Mickey exclaimed. He slapped me across the back really hard. "Congrats, dude."

"Are you ready for your first dare?" Morty asked. It wasn't a question — it was a threat.

"No," I said.

"Wh-what do we have to do?" Amanda stammered.

Mickey's grin finally faded. He shook his head. He stared hard at Amanda and me. "You're not going to like it," he said softly.

A blue-and-white city bus rumbled past. I saw a kid in a red cap staring out at us from a back window. If this were a movie, I'd grab Amanda's hand and we'd dart across the street. We'd chase after the bus and leap inside. And watch the Klass brothers back on the sidewalk, scratching their heads.

But this wasn't a movie. I watched the bus turn the corner and disappear.

"Here's your first dare," Mickey Klass said. "It's an easy one. Too easy."

"Well, maybe we'll come back when you have a harder one," I said. I started to walk past them, but Morty grabbed the front of my coat and shoved me back.

"We dare you to go through that gate," Mickey said, pointing. "And follow the path through the graveyard to the other side."

"Easy," Morty said, wiping his runny nose with the back of his hand.

Amanda and I gazed at the rusted iron gate that opened into the cemetery. I wondered if the Klass brothers knew that walking in the cemetery was our biggest fear.

We had to pass the graveyard twice each day, to and from school. We always walked *around* it. A lot of kids took a shortcut through the graves to the other side. Those were the kids who did *not* have bad nightmares about walking in the graveyard. Those kids did not include Amanda and me.

Amanda and I glanced at each other. I shivered. It wasn't from the cold. It was from fear.

"I . . . don't think I can do it," I told the Klass brothers. "I didn't bring the right shoes. My mom will kill me if I get these shoes muddy."

Morty raised his big boot and stomped as hard as he could on the toe of my shoe. When he removed his boot, he'd left a big mud stain on my shoe.

"Morty and I are going to watch you the whole way," Mickey said. "We want to see if a dead person reaches up from underground and grabs your legs and tries to pull you down."

Another one of my most frightening nightmares. *How did he know?*

It was Amanda's turn to shiver. "If a dead person tries to pull us into a grave," she said, "will you two come rescue us?"

"No way," Morty said. "We'll just laugh."

"Yeah, it'll be funny," Mickey agreed.

"Ha-ha," I said.

Morty gave me a shove toward the gate. "Stop stalling. We dared you to walk through the graveyard. So . . ."

"Maybe I could do it tomorrow?" I said. "I don't feel right disturbing the dead on a weekend."

Mickey and Morty squinted at me. They were both wheezing now, breathing hard. That's how you could tell they were angry.

"Sunday is when the zombies come out," Morty said. "You want to see zombies — don't you?"

"Get going," his brother muttered.

I saw Amanda's shoulders slump. She knew we had no choice. We had to walk through this frightening place we had been avoiding for months and months.

"We'll walk fast," I whispered to her. "It'll be okay."

The Klass brothers pushed us along the low wall to the iron gate. Mickey grabbed the end of the gate and shook it hard. It rattled and creaked, and opened just enough for Amanda and me to slide through.

"Good luck," Mickey said. I felt his big hands on my back as he gave me a hard shove — and I went stumbling into the graveyard.

5

I could hear the Klass brothers laughing on the other side of the gate. Amanda brushed dead leaves off the front of my coat. "We can do this," she whispered. "We'll follow the path. Nothing will happen."

"B-but where is the path?" I stammered. I gazed all around. The white gravestones tilted up through the carpet of leaves like hundreds of teeth.

"I guess the path is covered with leaves," Amanda said. "Let's just climb that hill and get away from the Klass brothers."

The carpet of dead leaves cracked and crackled under our shoes as we lowered our heads to the wind and began to climb the low, sloping hill. Gravestones poked up on both sides of us.

I tried to keep my eyes straight ahead. We walked side by side. Neither one of us wanted to be the leader.

A low groan made me stop. I grabbed Amanda's sleeve. "What was that?"

She squinted at me. "What was *what*?"

"Didn't you hear that groan? Sort of like a long moan? Like a human groaning? You didn't hear it?"

She shook her head. "Keep walking, Scott."

We reached the top of the hill. A tall, dark tombstone stood in front of us. The top was cracked, the stone split. And the words that had been inscribed had been rubbed off by time. It was just a smooth black stone.

"We . . . we're standing on top of someone," I murmured. "Every step we take, we're standing on top of people's bodies."

"Don't think about it," Amanda scolded.

"Don't think about it? I'm already thinking about it," I said. "What else can I think about?"

I gasped when I heard the groan again, a deep throaty moan. I grabbed Amanda's sleeve. "Did you hear it? Did you hear it that time?"

She nodded. Her eyes were wide. "I heard it," she whispered.

We both stood frozen. Wisps of fog moved over the ground. The air felt even colder.

"Let's get out of here," she said. She turned and began to make her way along a narrow path through two rows of old graves. The fog swirled around us, making it hard to see. In the distance, tall trees bent and swayed against the cemetery wall.

And then I stopped. And gasped again. "Amanda —" I choked out.

Up ahead, I saw another tall tombstone. And someone moving. Someone crawling up from behind the stone.

"Amanda —" I said her name again. But I was too frightened to say any more. Her eyes were wide. She saw the figure, too. We both stared into the curtain of fog.

Stared at the figure climbing up from beneath the gravestone up ahead.

"It . . . it's a man," I stammered. I squeezed Amanda's sleeve.

My nightmare. Coming to life. Not a dream. My nightmare — suddenly *real.*

The man struggled to his feet. He brushed leaves off his long black coat. Then he came staggering toward us, walking so stiffly . . . as if he hadn't walked in years. Staggering, bent over, his arms rigid at his side.

Staggering through the leaves, through the swirls of gray fog.

And then Amanda and I both opened our mouths in screams of horror.

We both saw it. We both saw him so clearly.

The man had no head.

I stared at the collar of his black coat. Buttoned tight. But no head above the collar. No head.

He lumbered stiffly forward.

I tried to back away, but I stumbled over a low gravestone. With a sharp cry, I landed hard on my back. My breath rushed out in a loud, painful *whoosh*.

Amanda turned and reached for my hand. She tugged me to my feet. I struggled to catch my breath.

The headless ghoul was only a few feet from us. His shoes clumped heavily as he dragged them over the crackling dead leaves.

I opened my mouth to scream again. But I stopped when I heard laughter behind me. I turned and saw Mickey and Morty running through the gravestones, racing toward us.

Amanda squeezed my arm. "Scott — look."

I turned in time to see the headless zombie unbutton the collar of his coat. He tugged the coat down and a head slid up from beneath the collar. A grinning head I recognized immediately.

Kenji Kuroda.

Mickey and Morty's best buddy.

Kenji straightened his black hair with both hands. Then he tossed back his head and let out a *whoop* of triumph. He pumped his fists in the air and did a wild dance.

Mickey and Morty were laughing so hard they had tears running down the sides of their fat faces. "We didn't think you'd fall for it," Morty said. "Did you really think he had no head?"

"We have to find someone else to scare," Mickey said, wiping tears from his cheeks. "You two are too stupid. You're too easy."

"Yeah. We need a challenge," Morty agreed. "You're pitiful."

Kenji let out another *whoop*. Grinning, he slid his coat over his head again. "Ooh, look at me. I'm headless. I'm headless."

Mickey and Morty started heehawing all over again, shaking their heads and slapping their knees.

"I-I wasn't scared," I said. "No way."

They stopped laughing and squinted at me.

"I knew he wasn't headless. I was just playing along," I said.

Morty poked my chest with his stubby finger. "Is that why you fell over the tombstone, screamed, and called for your mommy?"

23

"He didn't call for his mommy!" Amanda exclaimed. "Maybe we both screamed a little, but . . ."

"We were acting," I said. "You know. Trying to be funny — ERRRRRK!"

I let out a squawk because Kenji had sneaked up behind me and squeezed the back of my neck as hard as he could.

He grinned at me. "You sounded just like a goose. Do it again."

"Give me a break," I muttered. My hands were clenched into tight fists. I suddenly pictured a big fistfight. I slam Mickey in the jaw and he sinks to his knees, moaning. Morty lunges at me, but Amanda drives both of her fists into his stomach, and he drops like a sack of meat. I land a hard punch on Kenji's head and he does a backflip and sprawls, helpless, on the ground.

And then Amanda and I use the three of them as punching bags. Punching . . . punching . . . punching . . .

I've never actually punched anyone. Not even Rita, although she punches me all the time. I think it would probably hurt my fist. I don't like to bleed. And, of course, if I started a fight with these three hulks, they would pound me into the ground and put a tombstone over my head.

Now Amanda and I watched as the three dudes walked away, hitting each other's shoulders, heehawing and enjoying their victory.

I turned and saw Amanda staring at me. Studying me. I had the sudden feeling that even *she* was embarrassed for me.

"*You* believed it, too," I snapped.

"Scott, I didn't say a word," she replied.

"I saw the look on your face, Amanda. You believed that Kenji was headless, too. I know you did."

She stuck out her chin. "Maybe...and maybe not."

I gazed around the graveyard. My eyes landed on the old abandoned house in the distance. "I hate this graveyard. I hate that house. I hate this *whole neighborhood,*" I declared.

"Don't go crazy," Amanda said softly. "We'll find a way to pay those three creeps back."

"You're joking, right?" I said. "Pay them back? That's not what I'm worried about."

"What are you worried about, Scott?"

I shook my head. "I'm worried about what they're going to do to us next."

"Where've you been?" Mom asked when I got home. She sat at the kitchen table, snapping snow peas into a big orange bowl. Mom loves snapping things . . . peas . . . string beans . . . whatever she can snap.

"Just hanging out with Amanda," I said.

"Your dad called from Germany. He's in Frankfurt now," she said. "He said to say hi."

"When is he coming home?" I asked. I leaned over the table, picked up a handful of snow peas, and snapped them for her.

She shrugged. "In a couple of weeks, I think."

Dad travels overseas a lot. He works for a hedge fund. I've asked him a million times what that means, but he can't explain it. I only know it has nothing to do with hedges.

Mom stood up and pushed back her chair. "If you snap the peas, I can peel the potatoes."

"Okay," I said. As I started to lower myself into the chair, she ran a hand through my hair.

"Scott, how'd you get all these leaves in your hair? You weren't rolling on the ground, were you?" She pulled out two or three dead leaves.

"Huh? Why would I roll on the ground?" I said. "I guess the wind blew them there." I leaned over the orange bowl and started to snap peas.

A few seconds later, Rita burst into the room, giggling. She wore a dark-green smiley-face T-shirt over bright-yellow shorts. Even in October. She always dresses like it's summer.

"What's so funny?" Mom asked. She turned from the sink, where she was starting to peel the potatoes.

"You have to see this," Rita said, grinning so hard I thought her dimples might pop right off her face. She held up her iPad. She turned to me, her blue eyes sparkling. "Scott, why were you and Amanda in the graveyard?"

"Huh?" My heart skipped a beat. "How do you know that?" I demanded.

She waved the iPad in front of me. "I saw you there."

I jumped up. "What do you mean?" I tried to grab the iPad from her hand, but she snatched it out of my reach.

Mom walked over, drying her hands on a towel. "What is it?"

Rita had a very evil expression on her face.

27

"Watch," she said. She held up the screen and pressed PLAY.

I gasped as I saw Amanda and me standing in the graveyard.

"It's a YouTube video," Rita said. "The Klass brothers just put it up."

"Turn it off! Give that to me!" I cried.

On the screen, I saw Kenji in his black coat. It looked like he was climbing up from a grave. He came staggering toward the camera.

Rita giggled and raised the screen to Mom. "Watch this part."

I heard Amanda and me scream. Mom started to laugh along with Rita as I toppled over the grave and fell on my back, shrieking and whimpering in fright.

Kenji loomed over us, headless. The big black coat filled the screen.

The video ended. Mom and Rita turned to me.

"We were pretending," I said. "It was like a movie. You know. We weren't really scared. We were all making a horror movie."

"You looked pretty scared," Mom said.

Rita raised the iPad. "Let's watch it again."

"No way," I said. I grabbed it from her hands. "I can't believe the stupid Klass brothers put that on YouTube."

Rita grinned, dimples popping again. "Everyone is going to see it," she said. "Everyone in school. They're all going to see it." She giggled. "You're doomed."

Rita has a scary sense of humor, am I right? The scariest thing about it is that she was *right*.

I just didn't know how *doomed* I was.

Upstairs in my room after dinner, I watched the YouTube video a few more times. Would kids at school believe me when I said it was all a joke? That Amanda and I were pretending to be scared?

Probably not. They knew us too well.

I thought about never going to school again. That would definitely solve the problem. But . . . it might cause a few other problems with Mom and Dad.

My brain spinning in my skull, I settled down at my desk to read my history assignment. It had something to do with paper drives, people collecting spare newspapers during World War II.

I couldn't concentrate. I didn't know what I was reading. And then the frightening sounds started, and I totally lost it.

Squeak . . . squeak . . . squeeeeeak . . .

I jumped to my feet, knocking over my desk chair. An animal in my room? What kind of animal would make that creepy squeaking sound?

It had to be a rodent of some kind. A *large* rodent. Maybe with long, curled teeth poking from its hungry mouth.

I gazed around, feeling the panic push my dinner up from my stomach. And then, a few seconds later, I laughed. I saw the creature making that sound.

I could feel myself blushing. *Scott, what is your problem?*

The squeak was Hammy, my hamster, running on his plastic wheel.

Oh, wow.

Scott, dude, you have got to CALM DOWN. Every little squeak makes you jump in fright.

I took a deep breath. I raised my right hand and took a vow. "I will stop being scared of my own shadow." I said the words out loud.

I picked up my desk chair and sat back down. I leaned over the desk and tried to find my place in the history text.

And that's when the *thumps* started.

THUMP . . . THUMP . . . THUMP . . .

Like a big fist pounding on wood.

Definitely not Hammy.

THUMP . . . THUMMMP . . .

Nearby. In my room. So close. I slammed my history book shut. I froze with my hands gripping the desk chair arms. And listened.

THUMP . . . THUMPTHUMP.

And behind the loud thumps, I heard a low

31

ghostly moan. Soft at first, then rising like the wind.

Once again, I jumped to my feet. I turned to my clothes closet. "Rita — I know it's you," I called.

Silence.

"Come out of there," I demanded. "You did that thumping thing before. Remember?"

Silence.

And then, THUMP . . . THUMP . . .

I crossed the room to the closet, my eyes on the door. "Rita, seriously, I know it's not a ghost. Okay, it worked the first time. You scared me once. But you're not going to scare me twice."

Silence.

I clenched my fists. "I have homework to do. This isn't funny. Come out — right now. I'm warning you."

Silence.

"Okay." I grabbed the doorknob. Turned it and jerked the closet door open. "Rita?"

No one in there.

The closet is very wide and filled with my clothes from one end to the other. I poked my head in and shoved some shirts on hangers out of the way. "Rita?"

Some sweaters and old winter coats blocked my view. I edged into the closet and tried to push them aside. "I know you're in here, Rita."

I forced myself deeper into the closet. But I couldn't see her.

A heavy coat fell off its hanger and dropped over my head and shoulders. I struggled to slide it off. It was like I was wrestling with it. Finally, I managed to free myself. I let the coat fall to the floor, and I backed out of the closet.

Silent now. No thumps or moans. I shut the door carefully, making sure it clicked.

I stood there staring at the closet door. "It *has* to be Rita," I murmured to myself. "Who else would be thumping inside my closet?"

I decided that if it started up again, I'd just ignore it. Let her stay in there till she got tired of her little joke.

I returned to my history assignment. But, of course, I couldn't concentrate. I kept waiting for the thumps to start up again.

And they did.

THUMP . . . THUMP . . .

I dove across the room and heaved open the closet door. "Rita? Is it you?" My voice cracked.

I heard a cough.

"I hear you," I cried. "I know you're in here."

It was a very deep closet. I shoved a long row of shirts on hangers to the side and peered way to the back.

No one there.

"Rita? Where are you?"

Then, near the back wall, I saw something move on the floor. I lowered my eyes to the old sleeping bag I used for day camp. Something wriggled inside.

"Caught you!" I cried.

I bent down, grabbed the end of the sleeping bag with both hands — and tugged hard.

She came sliding out headfirst.

I blinked. And let out a startled cry.

"Amanda? Huh? What are *you* doing in here?"

She wriggled out of the bag. Her hair was wet, matted against her head, and her face was beet red. She kept her eyes down, avoiding my face.

"I repeat," I said. "Why are you in my closet, making creepy sounds and trying to scare me?" My voice cracked. I was still in shock. I couldn't believe it was Amanda and not Rita.

"I-I," she stammered. She still didn't raise her eyes. "They . . . made me."

I backed up into my room, and she followed me out of the closet. She brushed back her hair with both hands. She wiped sweat off her forehead with the back of one hand.

"Who made you?" I demanded.

"Mickey and Morty," she said, finally looking me in the eyes. "They stole my backpack. They said they'd toss it in Grasswoods Creek unless I did what they told me to do."

"And they told you to sneak into my house and scare me?" I said.

Amanda nodded. "They said if I scared you and snapped a picture of your frightened face, they'd give me back the backpack." She tossed her hands in the air. "It's not like I *wanted* to scare you, Scott."

"But why didn't you tell me about it first?" I cried. "I would have made a frightened face for your picture."

She swallowed. "I . . . didn't think of that. I was so desperate to get my backpack from them, I couldn't think straight. Also, I forgot my phone — I don't have a camera. Can I borrow yours so I can take your picture?"

I scowled at her. Then I uttered a frustrated cry and dropped onto the edge of my bed. "Why does everyone want to scare me?"

"Because it's *fun*?" a voice chimed in from the doorway. Rita came prancing in with her iPad in one hand.

"Did it work?" she asked Amanda. "Did you scare him?" Rita turned to me. "I helped. I let Amanda into the house."

"Sorry." Amanda shrugged. "Someone had to let me in."

"Go away, Rita," I muttered. "I am definitely not in the mood for you," I said.

She stuck out her tongue. "I'm not in the mood for you, either, Scott," she snapped. "But I just saw that you wet your pants when you were in the graveyard this afternoon."

"Huh?" I leaped to my feet. My jaw dropped open, down to my knees. "What are you talking about?"

She raised her iPad in front of her. "Mickey Klass put it on his Instagram a few minutes ago," she said. "Look." She pushed it into my face.

I saw a picture of me on my back in the grave-yard with Kenji standing over me in his black coat. The caption read: "Scott wet his pants when he saw the headless zombie."

"That's a LIE!" I shrieked. "That's a total lie! I didn't wet my pants. He put this on his Instagram? First the YouTube video, and now *this*?"

"The whole school will see it," Rita said. "They'll believe it, too."

"Get OUT!" I screamed. "Get out of my room!"

Amanda put a hand on my arm. "Don't blame her. It's not Rita's fault."

"But she's enjoying it too much," I said.

I pushed Rita out of the room and shut the door. Then I began pacing back and forth in front of Amanda, clenching and unclenching my fists.

"What are we going to do? What are we going to do?" I murmured over and over. I stopped pacing. "I know. We'll call the police. The Klass brothers are thieves, right? They stole your backpack."

Amanda shook her head. "Scott, take a deep breath. Think for a minute. If we call the police on them, how will Mickey and Morty react? It will make them angry, right? And when they're angry, how will they treat us?"

I thought about it. "Worse? A lot worse? A hundred times worse? *Two* hundred times worse?"

"You've got it," she said. "If you think they're bad now . . ." Her voice trailed off.

"Okay. You're right," I said. "No police." I started pacing back and forth again. "What if we force their parents to send Mickey and Morty away to school?" I said. "Or what if we force their parents to move? To leave town?"

"That sounds a little difficult," Amanda said. "In fact, it's crazy. You're not thinking clearly, Scott."

"You're right," I said. I was breathing so hard, my heart was pounding in my chest.

"I've got it!" I cried. "We can get Wolverine. I know we can. He'll come and just rough up the Klass brothers a little. You know. Scare them. He doesn't have to punch out their lights. He could just scare them. No. Wait. It wouldn't have to be Wolverine. He's too big a star. It could be someone else. Not as important. Maybe one of the Guardians? Or . . . or . . . it could even be Ant-Man. And —"

Amanda grabbed me and forced me to stop pacing. She led me to the edge of the bed and pushed me down. "Calm your brain, Scott. You've gone a little berserk. Those characters aren't real — remember? Remember?"

"But we need a plan!" I cried. "We can't go on like this. We need a good plan!"

"That's what we need," Amanda said softly. "A good plan."

Wouldn't you know it? We had a good plan a few days later.

PART TWO

10

In school on Monday morning, kids I passed in the hall gave me big smiles. I knew why they were smiling. Because of Mickey Klass's Instagram.

I smiled back. I pretended I didn't know anything about it.

The main hall was more crowded than usual. Some kids were on ladders, putting up Halloween posters and banners.

Mr. Duffy, the art teacher, was darting back and forth, directing traffic, telling kids where every poster should be hung. Everyone likes Mr. Duffy. He's big and round and jolly, and wears these insane bib overalls every day. The only problem is, he's a total control freak.

"Wait right there, Scott," he said, holding me back by the shoulders. "Wait till we get this banner up straight. Don't walk between the ladders."

"No problem," I said.

Halloween. My least favorite time of year.

Yes, I know. Most kids love Halloween. They love the costume parties and the candy and all the scary movies they show day and night on TV.

You may have guessed that I'm not a scary-movie guy.

But my big problem with Halloween is Mickey and Morty. They think the whole point of the holiday is to go wild and scare Amanda and me to death.

Last year, they stopped us on the way to a costume party. They took our cell phones and actually forced us to climb up onto a high limb of a tree overlooking the elementary school playground. Then they left us there.

Amanda and I were freezing to death in our costumes, clinging to the tree limb for dear life. Could you guess that we're not good at climbing down trees?

I have a problem with heights. I get dizzy looking down at my *shoes*.

It was a windy night and the limb kept creaking and swaying, making cracking noises like it was going to break off.

We were terrified and freezing and terrified. Did I mention *terrified*?

Finally, a man came by in an SUV full of kids he was taking to a Halloween party. He spotted Amanda and me up there, stopped his car, and rescued us. We found our cell phones on the ground, tilted against the tree trunk.

The man asked how we got stranded up there. We were afraid to tell him about the Klass brothers. We told him we lost a bet.

That was last year. I had nightmares late at night about what the Klass brothers planned to do to us *this* Halloween.

Kids were moving the ladders down the hall. They had one more orange-and-black banner to put up. A kid in my class, Jerome Jackson, grinned down at me from the top rung of a ladder. "Hey, Scott — I saw your picture!" he shouted. He laughed and a bunch of other kids laughed. The entire hall rang with cruel laughter.

Scott, you can get through this, I told myself.

I spotted Mickey Klass in front of the music room, and I stopped and pressed my back against the wall. He was talking to the two most awesome cheerleaders in our school, Rosie McGregor and Luanna Jones. He was gesturing with both hands and making funny faces, and they were tossing their heads back and laughing.

Was he telling them about Amanda and me?

Whatever he was telling them, they were really into it. I could see that Mickey was doing everything he could to impress them. And as I watched, something inside me snapped.

And I decided it was time. Time for a little payback. Time to start paying Mickey back for all the bad times he had given Amanda and me.

My idea flashed into my mind as I watched the two cheerleaders grin and laugh and shake their heads at his story.

We have a dress rule in our school. Boys can't wear baggy jeans that sag down low so everyone can see your boxer shorts. Only regular jeans are allowed, and they have to be held up by a belt.

A lot of kids don't like it, but it's a school rule. And Mr. Lundy, the vice principal, is in charge of enforcing the dress code.

But somehow Mickey and Morty ignore the saggy jeans rule completely, and they never get caught or sent home or anything. I don't know how they get away with it. Maybe Mr. Lundy is afraid of them, too?

Mickey was teasing Luanna now. He tugged her long black hair, and she laughed. I started to creep closer. My eyes were on Mickey's baggy, faded jeans. They sagged way down, and you could see his black-and-white-striped boxers.

One tug, I thought. *One hard tug and the pants go down to the floor.*

Yes. That was my plan. Simple, right? I intended to pants Mickey in front of the two most awesome girls in school.

It was a simple plan but a good one. Because I knew at lunch today, kids in the cafeteria wouldn't be talking about the photo of me being terrified in the graveyard. They'd be talking about how I pantsed Mickey in front of Rosie and Luanna.

I knew I'd be the hero of the story, and he would be the total fool.

Ha-ha-ha-ha-ha. I wanted to laugh out loud, but of course I didn't. If I laughed, I wouldn't be able to sneak up behind Mickey.

Which I did.

I crept up behind him. Lowered my hands — reached for the back of his jeans.

And let out a startled scream.

11

I felt a hard tug at my waist. I stumbled. Almost fell.

It took me a few seconds to realize my jeans were down around my ankles.

Rosie and Luanna shrieked. Their eyes went wide and they started to roar with laughter. Mickey had this big dumb grin on his face.

I think I stopped breathing. I think time stopped and the world froze.

It all didn't seem real.

Until I spun around and saw Kenji Kuroda standing behind me. And a few seconds later, my brain clicked in, came back to life, and I knew that Kenji had figured out what I planned to do — and pantsed me.

Pantsed me in the crowded main hall in front of the two most awesome cheerleaders in school.

And why? Why, I ask you? Why of all days did I choose this day to wear the Hello Kitty boxers my grandmother gave me?

You can't imagine the laughter that echoed down the hall. Kids on ladders were laughing. A big crowd gathered around us. Kids giggled and pointed and slammed their hands against lockers and hooted and cheered and slapped their foreheads and made jokes about Hello Kitty.

Luanna was in hysterics. She laughed so hard she started to choke. Rosie had to help her to the girls' bathroom.

"I had no choice. I had to wear these!" I shouted over the laughter. "The others were all dirty!"

Lame, right?

That made everyone laugh even harder.

Then, suddenly, the laughter was shut off. Like someone had turned off a TV or pushed STOP on a song they were listening to on their phone.

The long hall was hushed in a strange silence.

I turned and saw why the laughing and hooting had stopped. Vice Principal Lundy stood with his hands pressed against his waist, his eyes lowered to my jeans. My jeans wrinkled around my ankles on the floor.

"Scott?" His high whistle of a voice echoed off the rows of lockers. "Do we have a problem here?"

"Uh . . . not really," I choked out. I started to pull up my jeans. Looking up, I saw that Mickey and Kenji were nowhere to be seen. They had vanished at the first sight of Mr. Lundy.

"Did someone do this to you?" Lundy demanded, hands still pressed tightly on the waist of his brown suit pants.

"Uh . . . no," I lied. "I guess I need to wear a belt."

He scrunched up his face. "Well . . . a belt might help. But, if I may say so, you might want to show better taste in boxer shorts."

The hall rang with laughter. The laughing was so loud, I think I saw the walls shaking.

And that's when I decided that Amanda and I had to return to that frightening abandoned house. That's the exact moment I knew we had to go back there.

Why?

I'll explain later.

12

Saturday morning, Rita came downstairs for breakfast in her winter parka. "Are you cold? Why are you wearing that?" Mom asked.

Rita shuddered. "There's a huge wasp upstairs. It's humongous. I tried to swat it with a magazine. But I made it angry. I put on my coat so it couldn't sting me."

I set down my cereal spoon. "A wasp in October? Expect me to believe that?"

"You'd better believe it," Rita said. "I chased it into your room and I closed the door."

I jumped to my feet. "Liar." This was typical Rita, trying to scare me first thing in the morning. She knows I have a thing about wasps.

Mom frowned at me over her coffee mug. "Why are you calling your sister names?"

I started to the stairs. "Because she's a liar. She's only trying to scare me, Mom."

"I didn't make it up. I swear." Rita raised her

right hand. Like I was supposed to believe her. A wasp in October. Sure thing.

I hurried up the stairs and down the narrow hall. The door to my room was closed. I grabbed the knob, pushed it open, and stepped inside.

I gazed all around. Yesterday's jeans and T-shirt were strewn on the floor where I'd tossed them. My backpack tilted against the closet door.

"Rita up to her old tricks," I muttered.

Then I heard a loud, steady buzz. A shadow moved. I dodged to my left as an enormous wasp dive-bombed my head.

The terrifying buzz rose in my ear as the big insect thudded against my cheek, then up toward the ceiling, preparing to dive again.

"I'm hit! I'm stung!" My voice came out in a shriek. "It got me!"

My knees started to fold. But I scrambled to my feet and darted to the door. I slammed it hard, the touch of the deadly insect still tickling my cheek.

I rubbed my face. No bump. No sting.

Okay. I went berserk. I overreacted a little.

I burst back into the kitchen. "Rita was right!"

My sister had a pleased grin on her face, dimples popping. She loves to see me in a panic. I don't know why she enjoys it so much. I try to be nice to her. Most of the time.

Mom sipped her coffee. She brushed a strand of hair off her forehead. "Did you really see a wasp?"

"It . . . it attacked me," I said. "It's *huge*."

"I'll take care of it," Mom said. "Sit down. Finish your breakfast, Scott."

"Sit down?" I cried. "How can I finish my breakfast when I was almost *assassinated*?"

Rita was still grinning. "What does that word mean? Assassinated?"

"Never mind," I muttered.

And that got Saturday off to a very bad start. Because this was the day Amanda and I decided to try again. To prove that we could be brave so we could stand up to the Klass brothers. And I don't think you could say that I showed a lot of bravery facing the wasp in my bedroom.

In fact, I was maybe a little bit of a wimp.

After breakfast, Mom opened my bedroom window and the wasp flew out. No biggie. I slid into my coat and hurried to meet Amanda at the old abandoned house.

The sun was out when I left home. But as I approached the graveyard and the house across the street from it, gray clouds floated overhead, and the whole world seemed to turn to shades of gray.

As I walked past the graveyard, I kept glancing all around. I expected the Klass brothers to step in front me and tell me that my next dare in the Dare Club was to be buried alive in an open grave.

They would do that. You know they would.

But no sign of them this morning. I think maybe their mom drives them to private Bullying Lessons on Saturday mornings. Just a guess.

Amanda was waiting for me in front of the abandoned house. Her parka was unbuttoned. She had a purple knit cap over her hair. She waved as I trotted up to her.

"How's it going?" I asked.

She shrugged. "Are we really doing this?"

"Of course," I said. "This time, we're going in. It's almost Halloween, Amanda. The Hulk Brothers are probably already planning what they're going to do to ruin the holiday for us. We've got to get tough."

She didn't answer. Her eyes were on the grave-yard across the street.

I turned. "See anything?"

"No. Nothing moving over there. No headless people walking around."

I laughed at that. I'm not sure why.

Amanda tugged at the sleeve of my parka. "Scott, what if this old house really is haunted? Everyone in town says it is."

I pulled out my phone. "Then we'll take pictures of the ghosts," I said.

She studied me. "You're in a brave mood today."

"I'm pretending," I confessed.

She slapped my shoulder. "I thought so." She gazed up at the dark windows above the first floor, at the ragged, tilted shingles with their paint peeling. "What if we go in there and we're never seen again?"

"Well . . . here's an idea," I said. "Maybe you should stop asking questions?"

She nodded. She played with the zipper of her coat, tugging it up and down.

A car rumbled by, loud country music pouring out from its open windows. The man and woman in the front seat gazed out at us as they passed.

"Come on, Amanda," I said. "We're going in. No more stalling."

I led her around to the side of the house. We had to step through some prickly bushes. A thorn ripped a line in my coat sleeve.

The shadow of the house fell over us. The air suddenly grew cooler.

I stopped in front of a low window near the back of the house. "Maybe I can push that window up, and we can slip inside," I said. My voice came out breathless, more from fear than from being out of breath.

"It's pitch-black in the house," Amanda said, eyes on the window. "That window must have a hundred years of dirt on it. I can't see a thing."

"We're doing this," I said. I grabbed the stone window ledge with both hands and hoisted myself up. It took all my strength, but I got my knees up on the ledge. Then I stretched my body up, raised my arms, and shoved the window frame.

"Yes!"

It resisted at first. I thought it was stuck. But I gave it a second try, and the dirt-caked window slid up. I pushed again, and it moved even more. The window was halfway up.

I turned back to Amanda. "More than enough room for us to drop inside," I said. "Follow me. I'm going in."

I squeezed the top of the window frame with both hands. Turned my body. Carefully. Carefully. And lowered my feet into the house.

My heart was pounding so hard I could hear my pulse in my ears. My shoes found the floor. I let go of the window. And stood up. Stood up inside the dark house.

And as I did, I heard a deafening sound. A horrifying, ghostly cry. A *screech* so nearby . . . so close to me in the darkness. A long, shrill *screech* so frightening it made me scream.

13

"Scott — what *is* it?" Amanda called from outside.

I squinted into the darkness, the screech still ringing in my ears. "I-I don't know," I stammered.

Amanda hoisted her arms onto the window ledge. I turned, grabbed her by the shoulders, and tugged her into the house.

Silent now, except for our wheezing breaths.

"Maybe it was a cat," I said, finally finding my voice. "Maybe I startled a cat when I dropped to the floor."

She stared at me. "A cat in an abandoned house? You mean . . . a *ghost* cat?"

"No. Stop trying to scare me. I'm scared enough as it is," I said. "You know, sometimes cats find a way into houses. A hole in the wall or something."

I turned and gazed around. We were in a kitchen. The windows were so thick with dirt that almost no light came in. I felt like we were surrounded by a deep gray fog.

Amanda slapped the sleeves of her coat. "Cold in here," she muttered. "Cold as the grave."

"Shut up!" I shouted. "Seriously. Stop saying things like that. It's an old, empty house, that's all. Of course, it's cold in here and the air smells rotten and it's caked with dust. But look. We made it inside, right? That was our mission, and we made it. So stop saying scary things."

"You don't have to shout," she answered in a tiny voice.

"Look at that old refrigerator," I said, taking a few steps toward it. "It's so small, and it doesn't have a freezer." The door hung open, tilted on one hinge. I saw dark puddles of things on the fridge shelves. I didn't want to think about what they were.

"There's a rusted old-fashioned-looking oven," Amanda said. "But no stove."

"Take my picture in front of the fridge," I said. "Quick. We have to take a lot of pictures to prove to everyone we were in here."

I started toward the fridge but stopped when my shoe sank into something soft. "Ohhh." I let out a moan. I tried to lift my shoe, but whatever I'd stepped in was thick and sticky.

"Ooh, what did you step in?" Amanda asked. "It smells *putrid*."

"I . . . don't know," I said. "I'll clean it off later. Be careful where you walk."

I stepped up to the fridge. My shoe made sticky sounds on the wood floor. I turned toward Amanda, and she snapped a picture with her phone.

The flash was so bright in the darkness, it blinded me for a second. I had orange circles in front of my eyes. "Let's check out the other rooms," I said.

I heard a low moan. Like someone groaning in their sleep.

"Amanda? Was that you?"

She didn't answer. Her eyes were wide with fright. We both stood totally still, listening hard. "That sounded human, right?" she whispered.

I shrugged. "Old houses groan," I said. "Haven't you seen any scary movies? The houses always creak and groan in those movies."

"How would you know?" she snapped. "*You* don't watch scary movies."

"I . . . I read about them," I replied. I waved my hand to signal her to follow me.

The floorboards squeaked under my shoes. "I'm not afraid to be in here," I said. "I knew we could be brave. After today, we'll be brave enough to —"

I didn't finish my sentence. Another long, low moan made me stop. And then I felt something wrap itself around me, my face, my coat, my whole body. Something wrapped around me. It covered my eyes. It clung to my nose. Covered my mouth.

I tore at it with both hands. It stuck to my fingers. I clawed at it, struggling to tug it off my mouth, pull it away from my face, tear it off my eyes.

Finally, I sucked in a deep breath and managed to croak: "It's *got* me! Help. I . . . I can't *breathe*!"

14

Amanda dove across the room toward me. With a cry, she began to tear at the disgusting sticky sheet over my face. "It's cobwebs," she said. "Stop screaming, Scott. You walked into a curtain of cobwebs."

She pulled the thick, dry strings off my face. I tore at the webbing that clung to my neck and the collar of my parka. "It's ... as thick as ... as ..." I started.

"As thick as hundred-year-old cobwebs." Amanda finished my sentence for me.

We tore and grabbed and tugged the sticky webs off. I took a step back. And glanced down. "Oh, wow." Thousands of dead insects were wrapped in the cobwebs.

"They're in my hair!" I screamed. I began slapping frantically at my head. "They'll crawl into my ears! Into my *brain*!"

"Calm down, Scott. They're dead."

"Dead bugs! Hundreds of them in my hair! Oh, wow. It itches!" I cried. "My face itches. My hair itches. I'm going to itch *forever*, I know it."

She pulled an enormous dead spider off my forehead. "Remember when we talked about being brave? Remember that part?"

"Okay, okay," I muttered. I shuddered. My whole body itched like crazy. Still pulling the sticky stuff off my face, I followed Amanda into the next room. "This must be the living room," she said. Shoes thudding on the bare floorboards, we crossed the wide room to the windows. Through the dirt-caked glass, we could see the graveyard across the street.

I turned and gazed around. The fireplace still had a pile of logs inside it. The logs were covered with dust. Above the fireplace, the mantel had cracked. One side hung down to the floor.

Some old ripped-up furniture was scattered around the room. A long couch and two armchairs with stuffing poking out from the cushions. And what did I see on the floor beside the couch? "Ohh, yuck." Was that a nearly skeletal corpse of an enormous rat?

"Something to add to my nightmares," I said. "Think there are *live* rats all over the house?"

"Dunno," Amanda muttered. "Over here. Take my picture." She handed me her phone. "By the fireplace."

"Do you want to hold the rat bones in the photo?" I asked.

"Shut up and take the picture. I . . . I'm starting to think we've spent enough time in here."

She struck a pose next to the cracked mantelpiece. As I walked closer, I smelled something really gross. Like rotten eggs. From under the couch, I think.

I held my breath and snapped her picture.

"Sit on the couch," she said. "I'll take your picture."

I gazed at the couch, with its mold-covered cushions. I inhaled the rotten egg odor again. "I . . . I don't think so. There's something dead under there."

"Oh, go ahead." Amanda gave me a push.

I stumbled toward the couch. The sour odor filled my nose. I stopped when I heard the howl.

Not an animal howl. A *human* howl. Like someone in pain, someone crying out for help. I froze. Another howl rose and fell. It seemed to be coming from the dining room.

With a startled cry, I turned to Amanda. "Did you hear that? Hey —"

Amanda was gone.

15

"Amanda? Hey — Amanda?"

I froze in panic. I tried to shout, but my cries came out as choked whispers.

"Where are you? Hey — Amanda? Where are you?"

I spun around, squinting hard, as if I could make her reappear.

I heard another long, sad howl, and a chill rolled down my back. As the howl faded, I heard Amanda's voice, muffled as if she was calling from a distance.

"Scott — *help* me! Hurry!"

I turned toward her voice — and spotted the missing floorboards in front of the fireplace. Like a hole in the floor.

"Amanda?"

"Get me out of here!"

I hurried across the room and peered down into the hole. I let out a gasp as I saw her down below, her head just beneath the floor.

"It's like a trapdoor in the floor," she said. "I was standing there, and it just dropped down."

She raised both hands. "Pull me out of here."

I grabbed her hands and started to tug, and the floor rose with her. The floorboards clicked back into place. Amanda leaped away from them. "Why did someone build a trapdoor in the living room floor?"

"Beats me," I said. "Hey, I was scared. You disappeared. I heard those howls and —"

"I heard them, too," she said. "Definitely not a cat. Someone doesn't want us in here. Let's go. We've been brave enough for one day."

Another howl rose like an ambulance siren, the mournful sound ringing off the bare walls.

I started to run.

"Look out!" Amanda's shout made me stumble to a stop. I realized at once I'd been running right back to the trapdoor in the floor.

I spun away and, lowering my head, darted out of the living room. I saw Amanda close behind me. "Wrong way," she said breathlessly. "We've got to get back to the kitchen."

I gazed around. Something was pulling me . . . pulling me to the room behind us. A dining room? A den?

Amanda motioned for me to follow her. But something tugged me. Something pulled me into the other room. . . .

And then I saw an object on a low table that made me freeze.

In the dim light through two tall windows, I squinted at it. A small box. A small box of polished, dark wood.

"Weird," I muttered to myself. The box was the only thing in the room not covered in a thick layer of dust.

It was about the size of a shoe box. The wood gleamed in the gray light.

I can't explain it. Something about the box tugged me closer, pulled me to it. I knew I should leave. My brain was telling me to get out of there as fast as I could.

But I couldn't help myself. I grabbed the box. I slid it off the table and tucked it under the arm of my coat. And then I spun away and began to run, following Amanda to the kitchen.

She already had one leg out the window. She slid her body out the opening and balanced on the stone ledge. Then she lowered herself to the ground.

I moved to the window, turned and edged one leg out and onto the ledge. The box nearly fell from under my arm. I grabbed it and pressed it tight to my waist and somehow managed to lower myself out the window.

When I hit the ground, Amanda and I ran.

The sun had come out, but the air still carried a chill. Two kids on bikes raced past the graveyard wall across the street. A brown UPS truck was double-parked at the corner.

Amanda and I ran full speed past everything and everyone. We didn't slow down at the corner. We just ran blindly across the street. As if we were being chased. As if that howling creature in the old house was coming after us.

I pressed the wooden box against the side of my coat. It made it awkward to run, but I stumbled and staggered forward.

We both reached my house, gasping for breath. I pulled open the kitchen door, and we burst inside. No sign of Mom. The basement door was open. Maybe she was downstairs. Amanda and I stood still, struggling to catch our breath. I still had the wooden box pressed against my side.

We climbed the stairs and made our way down the hall to my room. Through the windows, the late morning sun made everything glow orange. I set the box down on my desk beside my laptop, pulled my coat off, and tossed it onto my bed.

Amanda let her coat fall to the floor. She brushed back her hair with both hands. Her eyes were on the wood box. "Scott? Did you take that from the house?"

I nodded. "Yeah."

She squinted at me. "Why?"

I stared at the box. "I don't know. It was just . . . just a crazy impulse. You know. I didn't really think about it. I just took it. It was kind of, like, *asking* me to take it."

"Weird," she muttered. She reached out a hand to the lid, but quickly pulled it back. "It's creepy. I don't want to touch it. I mean, what's in it?"

"We'll have to open it to find out," I said.

She crossed her arms in front of her, as if shielding herself. "But what if it's something horrible? What if it belonged to that ghost or whoever it was, the one howling at us? Scott . . . what if it has a *curse* on it?"

I didn't have an answer to that question. I was feeling all weird. I mean, why *did* I take it?

"I think we've been brave enough for one day," Amanda said. "We went into the haunted house, and we have the pictures to prove it. The next time the Klass brothers try to be mean to us, we can show them who the *real* brave kids are in this neighborhood."

"So what are you saying?" I asked. "Don't open the box?"

"Why look for more trouble?" she replied, her arms still tightly crossed. "I don't think you should open it."

"But I can't just leave it sitting here," I said. "I can't just have an old wooden box on my desk and not know what's inside it."

"Then take it back where it belongs," she said.

"No way, Amanda. No way I'm taking this back into that house."

We both gazed at the box. Outside, a cloud rolled over the sun, and a blue shadow filled my room. I felt a chill at the back of my neck.

"I'm going to open it," I said softly.

"No, Scott. Don't."

She tried to brush my hand away. But something was forcing my hand forward. Something was pulling me like a magnet, almost against my will.

I grabbed the wooden lid and started to pry it open.

16

"OHH, NOOOOOOOO!"

A cry of horror escaped my mouth, a cry from deep in my throat.

I staggered back from the box as a thick purple mist shot out of it. The dark mist came spraying out like water from a fire hydrant, billowing to the ceiling and filling my room with a sour odor, a putrid odor of rot.

"Shut the box! Shut the box!" Amanda screamed.

But I staggered away from the foul-smelling mist, my fingers pinched over my nose.

Amanda dropped to her knees. She covered her face with both hands, trying to keep out the smell. "Is it poison? Poison gas?"

I couldn't stop gagging. I lowered my head and ran across the hall to the bathroom. I washed my face with cold water. I held my breath until my stomach was back in control. Then I hurried back to my room.

The purple fog had vanished. Amanda was still on her knees. Her cheeks glistened with tears. Her body trembled. I helped pull her to her feet. "That smell . . ." she choked out.

I glanced around. "The fog is gone," I said.

"It shot out the window," Amanda said, nodding her head toward my open bedroom window. "It's gone, but it still stinks in here."

"It . . . it must have been trapped inside the box for a long time," I said.

Amanda sniffed the front of my sweatshirt. "It's in your clothes," she said. "The smell. Mine, too. I'm going home and taking a two-hour shower." She shuddered.

The box sat on the corner of the desk, the lid open. I took a few steps toward it.

"Don't touch it!" Amanda said.

"Too late," I told her. "We already opened it."

I stepped up to it and peered inside. "There's a red scarf in there," I said. "A long red scarf, very silky."

Amanda stepped up beside me. She wrapped her fingers around the scarf and started to pull it out of the box. "Weird," she muttered. "It's in perfect shape. A perfect silk scarf."

"And it doesn't smell bad," I said. I glanced around the room, as if expecting the putrid purple fog to return.

"The scarf is wrapped around something,"

Amanda said. She dropped it back into the box. "Maybe we shouldn't unwrap it."

"We've gone this far," I said. "We can't stop now."

Amanda took a few steps back. Her eyes were on the rolled-up red scarf. "I . . . I'm scared. I think this could be something dangerous."

"Well . . . it's our day to be brave," I said.

I lifted the scarf in both hands. The material was silky but heavy. It was wrapped around something hard. The scarf was longer than I thought. It took me a few minutes to unwrap it all the way.

And then Amanda and I gazed at the object inside. "A mask," I said. "It's a wooden mask."

"It's so ugly," Amanda whispered. "It's the scariest mask I've ever seen."

The wooden mask was brown and red. Two slits had been cut out of the wood for eyeholes. The nose was raised and pointed. The mouth was turned down in a frightening scowl.

"What's that on its forehead?" Amanda asked, keeping her distance.

"It's another head," I replied. "The mask has a tiny head poking out of its forehead."

Amanda shuddered. "So, so ugly . . ." she murmured.

"It-it's a *death mask*," I stammered.

She blinked. "A *what*?"

"A death mask. My dad brought one home from Mexico last year. They have this holiday called *Día de los Muertos*, the Day of the Dead. My dad said they make these death masks for that holiday."

Amanda squinted at it. Her mouth dropped open. "Does it mean someone is going to die?"

I held the mask in both hands, squinting hard at it.

"I . . . I don't *think* so," I said.

17

The mask shook in my trembling hands. I stared at the open eye slits. Then my eyes moved up to the ugly, carved head — the size of a thumb — poking out from the forehead.

My head swam with questions. Why was this death mask tucked away in the wooden box, wrapped so tightly in the red scarf? What was that disgusting purple spray that shot out of the box?

I suddenly wanted to be far away from this strange mask. But my hand raised it . . . brought it closer to my face. My hand was lifting the mask closer — *as if it was being commanded by someone else.*

Try me on.

Try me on.

I heard a hoarse whisper inside my head. Was the mask communicating with me? Was a powerful force inside the mask trying to force me to cover my face with it?

I knew I had to fight it. I couldn't let it win.

But then I heard the words out loud: "Try it on!"

Nooooooo.

Not inside my head. A voice beside me: "Try it on!"

I screamed and dropped the mask on the floor. Its white painted mouth scowled up at me.

I heard laughter. Familiar laughter. I turned and saw Rita beside me. "Try it on!" she repeated.

"Get out of my room!" I shouted.

Her eyes flashed. "I made you really think that mask was talking. Admit it."

"You did not," I lied.

Amanda gazed down at the mask. She didn't say a word.

I realized my fists were squeezed into tight balls. I wanted to pound Rita. But mainly, I wanted to pound *myself* for always falling for her tricks.

Rita reached down to grab the mask from the floor. But I grabbed it first and held it out of her reach.

"Let me see it," she insisted.

"Go away," I said. "You know you need my permission to come into my room."

She stuck her tongue out at me and made a loud spitting noise. "*That's* my permission."

"You're not funny," I said. "You're pathetic."

"You're pathetic," Rita shot back. "Is that mask supposed to be you ... with a big wart growing out of your head?"

"Ha-ha. Remind me to laugh. You're so funny," I said. "And it's not a wart. It's another carved head."

"Where did you get it?" Rita demanded.

I exchanged glances with Amanda. "We're not telling," Amanda told Rita.

"You mean you *stole* it?" Rita said. "I'm telling Mom."

I sighed and rolled my eyes. "Give me a break."

"Is that your Halloween mask?" Rita demanded.

"It's not the kind of mask you wear," I told her. "It's the kind you hang on a wall."

She sneered at me, hands pressed against her waist. "Scotty, wouldn't you be scared to hang that on your wall? Scared it will give you the evil eye?"

My little sister was right. *No way* I wanted this ugly thing on my wall, staring at me night and day. But could I admit that? No.

"I'm going to hang it on that wall," I said, pointing. "That way, it will look out the open door into your room across the hall. We'll see if you like it."

"Like I care?" she said sarcastically. She shoved the death mask toward my face. "Try it on. Go ahead."

"I told you, it's not that kind of mask," I said.

"You're afraid? Try it on. Try it on, Scott." She pushed it to my face again.

"I don't want to," I said. "I . . ."

Amanda motioned to me. "Oh, go ahead. Give Rita a thrill."

"Huh?" I gripped the edges of the mask in both hands. The ugly little head grinned up at me from the forehead. My hands started to sweat on the mask.

"Try it on. Try it on," Rita chanted.

And once again, I felt a hard tug. I felt the pull of the mask.

Once again, it was as if my hands were no longer part of me.

They raised the mask, turned it face-out, and pressed it over my face.

18

The mask felt rough, scratchy, and warm against my cheeks. At first, I couldn't breathe. I started to panic.

But then it slid into place. I gazed out through the narrow eye slits. Beyond the mask, my room seemed to ripple, as if everything were underwater. It took a long time to focus. It was as if I were seeing everything from a distance.

Amanda and Rita finally came into view. "How does it feel?" Rita demanded.

I tried to answer her, but my voice was muffled behind the mask. I wanted to tell her that it was very warm in here and I felt far away. But for some reason, I couldn't get the words out.

And then the two girls seemed to fade away. They vanished . . . into a curtain of gray fog.

Oh, wow. Where did they go?

I blinked hard, trying to bring them back. And then I realized I could hear the echo of voices. Distant voices in a buzz of static. I couldn't make out the words.

And then Mom's voice broke through the strange sounds. She was shouting from downstairs. "Dinnertime. Come on down."

Amanda reappeared in front of me. "Dinnertime?" she said. "I didn't realize it was so late. I promised my mom I'd be home early to walk Curly." She gave me a wave and disappeared back into the gray mist.

"Amanda?" I finally found my voice. "Don't you want to stay for dinner?"

But she was gone.

I lowered the mask and followed Rita down the stairs and into the kitchen. We took our places across from each other at the table. The table was set for three since Dad was still away on his business trip.

Mom turned from the stove, a big yellow platter in her hands. "What's up?" she asked. "What were you two doing up there?"

"Checking out Scott's mask," Rita said.

I realized I still had the mask gripped tightly in my hand. I didn't want Mom to see it. I knew she'd ask where I got it. And I didn't want to tell her I'd grabbed it from the old, abandoned house.

Just think of how many questions my mom would ask if she found out Amanda and I had broken into that place.

I tried to hide the mask under the table, but I was too late. Mom already had her eyes on it.

She set the big platter down on the end of the table. "Scott, I made your favorite tonight. Stewed beef tongue."

"Huh?" I stared at the big pink tongue standing upright on the platter, and I almost gagged. "Mom — that's not my favorite," I said. "Why did you say it's my favorite?"

A huge, bumpy cow tongue? I could picture it in a cow's mouth. Why did Mom say that was my favorite? She'd never made it before. We never had a big pink tongue on the dinner table. *Never*.

Mom eyed me sternly. "Scott, you know you love cow tongue. You told me it's your favorite. And look what else we're having."

She carried a soup tureen to the table and began ladling out bowls of soup. "Oyster soup," she said.

I could see the big gloppy oysters in the soup broth. "Mom — the oysters . . . they're raw," I stammered.

"Of course they're raw," she said. "That's the way you eat oysters." She passed a soup bowl to Rita, who didn't say a word.

"But . . . they're like big slugs," I said. "Like eating slugs. Raw. It's totally gross."

"Scott, I made this dinner just for you," Mom said, frowning. "Try one. Just put it on your tongue and let it go down easy."

"Put a raw slug on my tongue?" Why was Mom acting so weird?

"Show Mom your mask," Rita said. I could see Rita was determined to get me in trouble.

I didn't have a choice. I held up the wooden death mask.

"That's interesting," Mom said. She stood at the end of the table with her electric knife, cutting the cow tongue into narrow slices.

"He stole it," Rita said. "He stole the mask and he won't tell where he got it."

Mom lowered the knife and squinted at me. "Scott? Is that true? Did you really steal that mask?"

"I-I-I," I stammered, trying to think of a good answer.

The phone rang. *Saved by the bell.*

Mom hurried across the kitchen to the wall phone. It was Dad, calling from his business trip.

"Where is Dad?" I asked.

"He flew to Neptune," Mom said.

Was that supposed to be a joke?

She turned her back on us and started to talk to him.

I reached across the table and grabbed Rita's arm. "You like being a snitch?" I said in a harsh whisper. I didn't want Mom to hear. "You think that's funny? Getting me in trouble?"

"Let go of my arm, Scott," she said.

"You know, it's almost Halloween," I said.

"And who is going to take you trick-or-treating if I refuse? You'd better be nice to me, Rita. Or I'll ruin your Halloween."

I let go of her arm. She grabbed her spoon, dunked it in her bowl, and shot a big splash of oyster soup across the table onto my sweatshirt. Then she splashed another spoonful onto my face. A slimy oyster landed on my cheek and slid down to my shirt.

She started to laugh, and I totally lost it.

"I . . . I wish you'd never been born!" I shouted.

I saw a puff of purple smoke in front of my eyes. And when the smoke cleared, *Rita was gone.*

19

"Huh?"

I gasped in horror, gaping at Rita's empty chair.

Oh, no. I did it. I wished her gone — and she's gone. This can't be true!

I didn't mean it. Really! I didn't mean it!

The kitchen seemed to fade into a curtain of purple fog. Mom's voice faded, too. I sank into the mist, sank into a swirling darkness, as if I was falling into a bottomless smoky pit.

Silence.

Then I felt a tug. "Take off the mask, Scott." Rita's voice.

I opened my eyes. Rita tugged the death mask off my face with both hands. She squinted at me. "Are you okay? I've been calling and calling you."

"You . . . you're *here*?" I stammered.

"Where else would I be?" Rita snapped.

Amanda was still in my room, too. She hadn't left for home. "You put that mask over your face,

83

and then it was like you couldn't see or hear us," Amanda said, standing beside my bed.

I squeezed Rita's arm. "You're real?"

"Stop acting like a jerk," she said. "Mom called us down to dinner, and Amanda has to leave."

I couldn't shake away Rita's disappearance. *What was real and what wasn't real?*

"Rita, didn't we already go down to dinner? Didn't you splash oyster soup in my face?"

She laughed. "What a good idea."

Amanda was studying me. I could see the fear in her eyes.

It all began to come clear to me. The dinner table thing didn't happen. When I pressed the mask to my face, I had a fantasy, like a dream.

The mask totally messed with my mind. It was like I entered a different world. Or maybe an alternate world, the kind you see in sci-fi movies.

Would I have been trapped in that world if Rita hadn't pulled the mask off?

I didn't want to find out.

"Give that back to me, Rita." I grabbed the mask from her hand. "This thing is dangerous."

Rita laughed. Amanda didn't.

"I'm hiding this away somewhere," I said, searching my room frantically. "Until I can get rid of it. I definitely want it out of sight."

Rita shook her head. "You're afraid of a dumb mask?"

"I know what I'm doing," I said. "And *you* keep away from it, hear me?"

She raised both hands. "No problem. Keep your stupid mask."

"What about the sleeping bag in back of your closet? It would be safe back there," Amanda said. I think she understood how I felt.

"Yes! Perfect!" I said.

"I'm out of here," Rita said, heading to the hall. "I'm going down to dinner. Hamburgers tonight, and I'm starving."

She went downstairs. Amanda made her way to the door. She stopped and turned back to me. "You okay?"

"Yes," I said. "Just got a little freaked by the mask."

"I'm going to put the pictures of us hanging out in the abandoned house on my Instagram tonight," Amanda said. "When Mickey and Morty see it, they'll totally freak." She pumped a fist in the air. "Respect!"

"Respect," I repeated.

When she was gone, I carefully wrapped the mask in the heavy red scarf. Then I ducked into my closet and pressed my way past my clothes, all the way to the back. I dropped onto my hands and knees, pulled up the top of the sleeping bag, and stuffed the scarf and mask as far down as I could reach.

Then I backed out of my closet and carefully closed the door. I felt better already, knowing the mask was out of sight.

In his glass cage, Hammy was running happily on his squeaking wheel. "You go, dude!" I shouted. And I hurried down to dinner.

I felt as if I'd turned a corner. As if I'd taken a big step toward being a braver person, brave enough to get revenge on the Klass Brothers and everyone who tortured Amanda and me.

Yes, I'd turned a corner.

Of course, I had no idea how much horror waited just around the *next* corner.

PART THREE

20

"I have exciting news," Mom said at dinner.

We were eating hamburgers, and the fried potatoes Mom makes that are cut as thin as potato chips but are even saltier. Rita tried to squirt ketchup across the table at me when Mom's back was turned. Otherwise, all was peaceful.

"Are we getting a dog?" Rita said. She had a dribble of hamburger juice on her chin.

"No. That's not my news," Mom said, motioning for Rita to wipe her chin. "You know your father is allergic to dog fur."

"Why can't we get one without fur?" Rita demanded.

"We've had this conversation a hundred times," Mom said, passing the potato dish to me. "How many more times do we have to have it?"

"A hundred," Rita said.

Mom made a disgusted face at her. "Don't you want to hear my news? Your aunt Ida is coming for a visit."

"*Who?*" Rita and I both said at once.

"Well, you don't know her," Mom said. "She hasn't been here since Scott was a baby."

"So who *is* she?" I asked, spooning another heap of fried potatoes on my plate.

"She's a very interesting woman," Mom said. "Actually, she's your father's aunt. She is a very well-known photographer. She travels all over the world for different magazines, taking photos."

"Cool," I said.

"So she's old?" Rita said.

Mom swallowed a mouthful of hamburger. "Old people can be fun and interesting. Did you know that, Rita?"

Rita shrugged and didn't answer.

"Anyway, your aunt Ida is a lot of fun. She has a million crazy stories about all the interesting places she's been. She'll be here in a few days."

"Is she bringing a dog with her?" Rita asked. Then she burst out laughing.

Mom shook her head. "You are so not funny." But she was smiling anyway. Anything Rita does is okay with her.

The next morning was picture day at school. A photographer was coming to take everyone's photo for the yearbook and a picture of our class.

I decided to wear my best sweater, a black V-neck, over a navy-blue T-shirt, and my new jeans, which were still stiff and uncomfortable but would photograph nicely for the class photo.

It was a warm morning for late October. The air felt heavy and wet. The street and sidewalks were still puddled with rain from the night before. The lawns glistened under the sunlight.

I crossed the street when I reached the graveyard. I turned, searching up and down Ardmore Road for Amanda. No sign of her.

I started to trot, eyes straight ahead. As you know, I like to get past the graveyard as fast as I can. "Hey!" I cried out as I ran into a deep puddle and splashed cold rainwater over the front of my new jeans.

Forget about looking awesome in the class photo today.

Some kids across the street started to laugh. Had they seen me splash myself?

I started to walk but didn't get far. Mickey, Morty, and Kenji blocked my path. Mickey grinned that big grin of his that makes you want to punch his face for about half an hour. "Hey, Scotty. What's up?"

"Not your IQ," I said. I thought it was pretty clever, but the three of them stared at me as if I were speaking Martian.

"Was that supposed to be a joke?" Mickey said.

"I know a good joke," Morty chimed in. "Who got covered in mud on school picture day?"

"Hey, listen, guys —" I tried to back away.

"We didn't finish the joke," Morty said. He had a toothpick bobbing between his teeth. Guess he thought it made him look tough. "You have to wait for the punch line."

"But *I'm* the punch line!" I exclaimed.

"Yeah. You got it," Kenji said. He grabbed me around the waist and struggled to lift me off the sidewalk. It wasn't much of a struggle. He's a big, powerful bruiser.

A car rumbled past. I wished I could jump into it and zoom away.

Mickey grabbed my ankles. His brother held me around the shoulders. The three dudes carried me across the street and through the cemetery gates.

"Hey, guys? What are you going to do?" I cried. My voice came out tiny and shrill, like a bird chirping. "Can we talk about this?"

"Sure. Go ahead and talk," Kenji said.

"We want you to have a good photo," Morty said. "Something to remember. I mean, a sixth-grade photo is a big deal, right?"

"We want yours to be special," Mickey said.

I struggled and squirmed. I tried to kick myself free. But these guys were just too strong.

"I really want an *ordinary* photo," I said in my little bird voice. "Nothing special. Seriously."

Those were the last words I said before they heaved me headfirst into an open grave.

I didn't see it coming. I landed flat on my stomach with a hard, squishy splash. My face sank into the wet mud on the grave floor. I started to choke. I couldn't breathe.

It took a few seconds to get over the shock of thudding into the deep, wet mud. I heard their laughter above me. Then it faded away. I could hear the rapid thump of footsteps as the three Hulks took off, their mission accomplished.

I forced myself to my knees. I wiped a thick clot of mud from my eyes. Then mopped my face with the sleeve of my best sweater. Mud clung to the front of the sweater and both legs of my jeans. I raised a hand and brushed the thick gooey stuff from my hair.

"They call me Mud-Man!" I exclaimed. My voice echoed off the walls of the grave.

I pictured myself as a Marvel superhero — Mud-Man! — with an exclamation mark. A lot like the Hulk, or maybe as quiet and powerful as Thor. Mud-Man! I'd follow my three enemies to school and we'd have an all-day battle. And at the end, I'd force them to *eat their weight* in mud!

Yesss!

But that fantasy quickly evaporated. And I was left in the muddy swamp of a grave. Just a mud-caked sixth grader on school picture day. A victim once again.

Victim. What a sad, ugly word.

I shook my mud-soaked fist. *That's the last time. I'm not going to be a victim again.*

I glanced around, my brain spinning. Should I go on to school and tell everyone I was in an accident? Should I go home and change so I could take a decent photo in clean clothes?

I swallowed hard. I was so caked in mud, I could *taste* it on my tongue, smell it in my nostrils.

I gazed up at the clear blue sky. Then I lowered my eyes to the grave wall.

And I realized my horror-filled morning wasn't over.

Because I saw that the grave was *too deep.*

No way I could climb out.

21

Shall I skip the part where I claw and kick and strain and push and pull and fall and scream and slide back onto the muddy grave floor? Shall I forget about the part where my heart pounded so hard that my chest hurt, and I tore off all my fingernails, and the mud filled my sneakers and made me seem to weigh two hundred pounds?

You don't want to hear every detail, do you?

You don't want to hear about me cold and shivering and soaked through with mud and freezing rain water. And you *definitely* don't want to know my thoughts while I was trying to climb out — because, believe me, they weren't pretty.

Let me just say that escaping from that grave took many tries. And when I finally crawled out, panting and wheezing, my tongue hanging out like an exhausted dog, I stayed there on my hands and knees for a while. I breathed the fresh, cool air and thought as many evil thoughts about Mickey, Morty, and Kenji as I could.

I slumped home, staying close to the houses, walking in the shade in hopes that no one would see me. Luckily, Mom had gone to work, so I didn't have to make any explanations. How could I explain that I'd spent nearly an hour rolling in mud in an empty grave?

It took me a while to decide where to hide my muddy clothes. Finally, I rolled them into a ball and shoved them into the back of my clothes closet underneath the sleeping bag. I knew Mom wouldn't find them there. The only problem was, how bad were they going to smell?

No time to worry about that. I took a fast shower, pulled on some clothes, grabbed my coat, and ran all the way to school. "Sorry I'm late," I told Miss Curdy. "I had to see my orthodontist."

That was the best excuse I could think of. I don't have an orthodontist, but almost everyone else in my class does. "Scott, open your mouth," she said.

I hesitated, then opened my mouth wide.

"You don't have braces," Miss Curdy said.

"I know," I replied. "That's why I had to see the orthodontist."

Later, I pulled Amanda to the back of the lunchroom. "We've got to talk," I said. "Desperate times."

She squinted at me and raised her lunch bag. "Scott, do you have lunch?"

I shook my head. "I don't care about lunch. We need to talk."

I found an empty table in the shadows at the back, and I dragged her over to it. I told her about my adventure in the graveyard this morning. She listened intently as she chewed her ham sandwich.

"*No más*," I said, repeating a slogan I'd heard in a TV commercial. "*No más*. They have to be stopped. No more Mr. Nice Guys. We need to hit them and hit them hard."

Amanda swallowed. Her face filled with surprise. "You mean with fists?"

"Of course not," I said. "But we need to put a stop to them. We need to get our revenge *now*."

"Any ideas?" she asked.

I didn't answer. At the far end of the cafeteria, I saw Mickey and Morty stride in. When they walked side by side, there was no room for anyone to pass. They were as wide as trucks. Real hairy, mean-looking trucks.

Morty grabbed a slice of pizza off a girl's lunch tray and gobbled it down. He and his Neanderthal brother slapped each other low fives.

"Scott? Any ideas?" Amanda repeated.

"We need to brainstorm," I said.

"Excuse me? What does that mean?"

"I don't know," I confessed. "It's something my dad says a lot. I think it means to think up ideas."

"Well, okay. Let's think. How can we scare the Klass brothers and Kenji?" Amanda rubbed her chin like she was thinking hard. "It's almost Halloween. . . ."

"Yes!" I exclaimed. "The scariest holiday of the year. We should definitely be able to scare them on Halloween." I thought hard. "Hmmmmmm. Hmmmmm." I thought harder. "Hmmmmmmm."

Amanda rested her chin in her hand and thought, too. "Hmmmmm."

"Hmmmmm. Hmmmmmm."

We were both humming away.

"I don't have a single idea," I said.

Amanda sighed. "Neither do I."

"I can't think clearly," I said. "I spent the morning trying to claw my way out of an open grave, and I'm just not thinking clearly."

"You still have some mud behind your ears," Amanda said, pointing.

I rubbed a finger behind my ear and felt a smear of dried mud.

"I know. We should have some kind of scary party," Amanda said. "You know. Invite Mickey, Morty, and Kenji. And then do everything we can to scare them to death."

"Like what?" I asked.

She shrugged. "I don't know. We're brainstorming — aren't we?"

"Wait. I know!" It was my turn to jump to my

feet. "I know! I know! I've got it. I know what will work. I know what will *terrify* them!"

Amanda's eyes went wide. "What? What *is* it?"

The bell rang. Right above our heads. It isn't really a bell. It's a long buzzer, loud enough to make your teeth rattle if you're sitting right under it, which we were.

No time to tell her my brilliant idea. We had to hurry to class. Loud voices rang off the tile walls. Lunch trays slammed. Kids trotted toward the cafeteria doors.

"Let's talk tonight," I called to Amanda. "After dinner."

She nodded and disappeared into the crowd of kids. I hung back. I saw the Klass brothers and Kenji were still at a table, gobbling up someone's lunch. I didn't want to run into them.

Believe it or not, I made it through the rest of the afternoon without any trouble. School picture day didn't happen. They told us the photographer got sick. Or maybe he broke his camera. I really wasn't listening. School picture day seemed like old news.

Finally, I had a plan to frighten the three cavemen and enjoy some revenge. I couldn't be bothered with unimportant matters like yearbook photos.

After school, I walked Rita to her piano lesson. Then I made my way home, plotting and scheming all the way. Mom wasn't home yet.

I carried my backpack upstairs — and stopped at the landing.

I heard strange noises. Scraping and bumping. Coming from my room?

I stepped up to the bedroom doorway — and gasped.

I gazed at a white-haired woman I'd never seen before. She was pawing through things on my dresser top.

She turned, startled to see me.

"Hey —" I blurted out. "Who *are* you?"

22

We stood there staring at each other. She had wavy white hair down to her shoulders. Her face was powdery and pale, and her skin was drawn tight against her cheeks. Her lips were gray. The only color on her face was in her bright blue eyes.

She wore a black outfit with a skirt that fell nearly to her ankles. She turned away from my dresser, a confused expression crossing her face.

Suddenly, I remembered. "Aunt Ida?" I cried. "You're Aunt Ida?"

"Yes," she said. "And you're . . ." Her voice was scratchy.

"Scott," I said. "You must be a little surprised. You haven't seen me since I was a baby."

She smoothed her white hair back with both hands. "Scott. Of course. Is this your room?"

"Yes," I said. "The guest room is down the hall. Let me show you." I motioned for her to follow me.

She glanced back at my dresser as we stepped into the hall. "I like your room," she said. "Funny. I remembered this house completely differently."

I stopped outside the guest room door at the end of the hall and waited for her to walk inside. I inhaled her perfume as she stepped past me. It was strong, very lemony.

Aunt Ida sat down on the bed and smoothed her long black skirt over her legs. "This is very nice." She smiled at me, and I saw something gleam, like a spark of light. It took me a few seconds to realize she had a gold tooth in the middle of her mouth.

Late afternoon sunlight washed in from the two windows. Before it became the guest room, this was my mom's sewing room. Her old sewing machine still stood in the corner, piled high with books and magazines.

"Mom says you're a world traveler," I said.

Her gold tooth gleamed again. "Yes, I am. I guess I'm a restless spirit, Scott. I can't stay in any one place for long." Her hands were long and bony. They played with the folds of her skirt.

"I bet you have some great stories," I said.

She nodded. "Some of them are so strange, I don't believe them myself." She shook her head. Her white hair shone in the sunlight.

"Can I help you bring up your suitcases?" I asked.

She hesitated. "They are being delivered. They are coming later."

"Would you like something to drink?" I was trying to be a good host. I wished Mom was home.

Aunt Ida climbed to her feet. Her long skirt rustled around her. "Actually, I have to go out," she said. Her blue eyes studied me for a moment. "I'll be right back. Give me a hug, Scott." She stretched out her arms.

I gave her a hug. I was startled by how bony her back felt, how frail. But she moved quickly to the stairs. "When I come back, we'll have a nice long talk," she said. "We'll get to know one another."

She made her way easily down the stairs. The smell of her lemony perfume lingered in the hall.

I carried my backpack into my room and tossed it against the wall. I took out my phone and started to text Amanda. I couldn't wait to tell her my idea for getting revenge on the three cavemen. But halfway through the message, I remembered Amanda was at her pottery class.

I dropped down at my desk and started to work on my science notebook. But it was hard to concentrate. For one thing, I could already smell the stale odor of my mud-caked clothes floating out of the closet.

I wished I knew how to run the washing machine. I could get my clothes clean while Mom was at work, and she would never have to know about the whole tragic incident.

But I didn't have a clue.

I bent my head over the notebook and tried to fill in today's assignment. But I felt a familiar pull. A strange force that made me climb to my feet.

I realized at once I was being pulled to my clothes closet.

The mask. I knew it was the mask. Calling to me again. Drawing me to its hiding place in the back of the closet.

No!

I knew I had to resist. But I had crossed the room. I wrapped my hand around the closet doorknob. I started to tug the door open.

I let go when I heard a door slam downstairs. "Mom? Is that you?" I called.

I forced myself away from the closet and hurried down the stairs two at a time. Mom was in the front hall, setting down her briefcase. She sells real estate in the Valley, which is a twenty-minute drive from home. She's usually pretty tired at night. Dad is the cook in the family. But since he's away on his business trip, Mom has to do everything.

She kissed me on the forehead. "Scott, how was your day?"

You mean the part where I was drowning in mud at the bottom of an open grave?

"Not bad," I said. "Picture day was canceled. Something happened to the photographer."

"Too bad," Mom murmured. She was sifting through the mail.

I opened my mouth to tell her that Aunt Ida had arrived. But she raised a hand and interrupted me. "Afraid I have bad news," Mom said. "Aunt Ida called me this afternoon. She's not feeling well. She's not going to visit us after all."

23

My mouth dropped open. It took me a few seconds before I could speak. "B-but, Mom —" I stammered. "There was a woman —"

The phone rang.

"I'll bet that's your father," Mom said. She dove for the phone. "Hi, Sid. Where are you now? Still in Berlin?"

I squeezed Mom's shoulder. "But I have to tell you something."

She waved me away. "Later, Scott. Your dad only has a few minutes to talk."

I sighed and slumped back upstairs to my room. My brain was doing flip-flops in my skull. I had a fluttery feeling in my chest.

An old woman was here. I hadn't imagine her.

I sniffed the air. The lemon perfume aroma had faded away.

Who was she? What was she doing in our house?

I dropped onto the edge of my bed, leaned forward with my hands clasped tightly in my lap, and tried to think. A few minutes later, I heard the door slam. Running footsteps on the stairs.

Had the old woman returned?

No. Rita peeked into my room. She had her coat half off. Her backpack strap was tangled in the sleeve. "Come here. I'll help you with that," I said.

She squinted at me. "Are you actually inviting me into your room?"

I nodded.

"Are you sick?" she asked, not budging from the doorway. "Do you have a horrifying flesh-eating disease you want to pass on to me?"

"Glad you trust me," I said. "I just wanted to help you with your backpack."

She crossed the room, and I untangled her. "And I want to tell you something."

"Uh-oh," she muttered.

Mom was on the phone. Amanda wasn't around. I knew I'd *burst* if I didn't tell *someone* about the old woman in our house.

"Listen to me," I said. "This is seriously creepy."

"Like the way you eat scrambled eggs?"

"Can you stop for one minute?" I pleaded. "I'm trying to tell you something." I squinted at her. "What's wrong with the way I eat scrambled eggs?"

"You suck them into your mouth. Like you're a vacuum cleaner. It's totally gross."

"I do not. Shut up about scrambled eggs. Listen to this. When I got home from school, there was an old woman up here."

That got Rita's interest. She sat down on the shag rug across from my bed.

"A strange woman in the house. She said she was Aunt Ida," I continued. "I found her in my room. She had white hair and looked really old and pale, like her skin was stretched across her face."

"Weird," Rita murmured.

"Very weird," I agreed. "I showed her to the spare bedroom. But she said she had to go out. And she hurried down the stairs and disappeared."

Rita rolled her eyes. "I don't get it, Scott. What's the big deal? Aunt Ida had to go out, and she'll probably be back soon."

"You *don't* get it," I said. "When Mom got home, she told me Aunt Ida got sick. She isn't coming."

Rita picked at the white shag rug with two fingers. I could see she was thinking about what I said.

"She was a creepy old woman, pale as a ghost," I said. "And she had a gold tooth right in the middle of her mouth. It glowed when she smiled."

And Rita burst out laughing.

I jumped to my feet and stood over her. "What's so funny?" I demanded. "Why are you laughing?"

She shook her head. "So lame," she said. "Seriously."

"Lame?" I cried. "What are you talking about?"

Rita jumped up and crossed her arms in front of her sweater. "Did you really think that lame story would scare me? Did you really think I'd totally freak and start screaming, *There's a ghost in the house*?" She gave me a hard shove backward with both hands. "You'll have to do better than that, Scott."

I gritted my teeth. I could feel my face getting hot. I wanted to grab her and shake. "It . . . it's not a story," I said. "She had bright blue eyes and — and —"

"And she flew out the window on a broom," Rita said. She laughed some more.

"And she reeked of this perfume," I said. "It smelled like lemon. It was so strong, it made my eyes water."

Rita sniffed a couple of times. "I don't smell anything. Except your armpits. Don't you ever take a shower?"

"Shut up!" I cried. "Shut up. I thought I could talk to you. For once. But I was wrong."

Rita picked up her backpack and started toward the door. "You thought you could scare me," she said. "But *I'm* the scary one in the family — not you. And now it's *my* turn."

"Huh? Your turn?"

She tossed her hair behind her shoulders. "My turn to scare *you*."

"But you've already had a million turns!" I cried.

She disappeared across the hall into her room.

I dropped back onto my bed. Shut my eyes and started to think again. I tried to remember every second I spent with the old woman. I pictured her in my room. And I realized she hadn't told me she was Aunt Ida. I asked *her* if she was Aunt Ida. And she simply said yes.

Why was she in my room?

I suddenly remembered the first moment I saw her. From the hallway. She was at my dresser. She was searching for something on my dresser. Maybe she had already gone through the drawers.

Searching for something . . .

I opened my eyes. I felt a chill roll down my back. I had a crazy thought. A totally insane thought.

The wooden box I took from the abandoned house. The death mask and the red scarf. Was she searching for them?

Did she come from that old house? Was she the one Amanda and I heard moaning and wailing?

Was she a ghost? And did that box belong to her?

She followed me home last Saturday. She waited for a school day. She came into my room to search for her belongings and take them back.

No. No way. It was too crazy.

Rita was right. Now I was inventing ghost stories. Now I was making up a ghost story and scaring *myself*!

But . . . would she come back? Would she keep coming back till she found what she was looking for?

Suddenly, I realized my hand was on the closet door again. I jerked the door open. I had no choice. The mask was pulling me . . . drawing me to it with incredible force.

Crawling deep into the closet, I shoved the filthy jeans and sweater aside. I pulled myself on my hands and knees to the back. In the dim light, I could see the sleeping bag against the wall.

I can't stop. I can't help myself.

I can't . . .

I edged my body forward and pulled the sleeping bag toward me. It was hard to see. I wished I'd remembered to turn on the closet light.

I tugged the sleeping bag around and reached my arm into the opening. My heart started to leap around in my chest, and I broke into an instant sweat.

I spread open the sleeping bag and forced my hand in deeper. And my fingers wrapped around the mask. I slid it out carefully and turned it to face me. Even in the dim closet light, I could see its grim expression . . . its angry scowl.

I couldn't help myself. I couldn't resist it.

I raised it closer, gazing at the ugly carved head poking from its forehead. And then I gasped as the mask spun in my hands and slammed itself over my face.

24

So warm. The wood of the mask felt as warm as human skin.

Once again, I heard voices rising and falling, distant voices in a drone of static. I gasped as I saw Amanda. She stepped forward from a billowing gray fog. Her eyes were wide. She had a smile on her face that I'd never seen before.

"Amanda?" I tried to call to her. But the mask was too tight around my face.

I could still feel the pull of the mask, drawing me inside, tugging my head, pulling me toward Amanda and the gray fog curtain behind her.

She raised a finger and signaled to me. *Come closer.* She was telling me to come to her. Her finger moved in slow-motion.

She had that strange smile on her face, frozen there, her lips glowing in the gray light.

"NOOOO!" A scream escaped my throat. "You're not Amanda! You're not the real Amanda!"

I knew the mask was making me see her. The mask was pulling me into a dream, like the dinner with the cow tongue and oyster soup.

"You're not real! I'm not coming to you. I don't want to be here. Let me OUT!"

I raised both hands to the sides of the mask — and pried it off my face.

Somehow I found the strength to pull it away, to fight the powerful force that was tugging me into the foggy world of the mask.

I gripped the mask in two hands, staring down at its ugly painted face. My hands were shaking. My whole body was drenched in sweat.

There's bad magic in this mask.

The words flashed through my mind as I struggled to catch my breath.

I knew I had to get the evil thing out of the house. But I *needed* it first. I needed it for my Halloween plan.

I wrapped it up in the long red scarf. Then I shoved it deep into the sleeping bag. I stuffed my muddy clothes under the sleeping bag and backed out of the closet.

I'll return it after Halloween, I told myself. *After the scariest Halloween party in the history of the world.*

After dinner, I phoned Amanda and told her my plan. At first, she thought I was crazy. But after I explained more, she agreed it was *bold*.

"It could work, Scott," she said. "It definitely could work."

That night, I couldn't get to sleep. I twisted and squirmed under the covers, then on top of the covers. I tried counting backward from a thousand. I even tried counting sheep, like in the cartoons.

But I was wide awake. Too many thoughts swirling around in my head. Too many crazy ideas.

And so, I was still awake late that night when the white-haired old lady returned to my room.

25

She appeared in the doorway to my room. Behind her, the hall was dark. But I could see her clearly in the blue light from my night-light.

Yes, I have a night-light. Maybe I mentioned that I'm not the bravest person in the world? Well, I don't see that it's a big deal to want a little light in your room in case you wake up during the night.

The old woman's hair was tinted blue in the light, and her pale face was almost completely hidden in shadow. Her long skirt rustled as she stepped into my room.

I kept my eyes open only a slit and pretended to be sound asleep. But I could see her clearly. She moved to my desk. Silently, carefully, she pulled open the top drawer. Then she slid it shut and tried the next drawer.

Was she looking for the mask?

I wanted to sit up and shout. I knew that would startle her.

But what would she do then?

A strong wave of fear kept me from moving.

In the pale glow from the night-light on the floor, I saw her expression. Tight-lipped. Angry. The blue eyes were black in the dim light. They gazed into the desk drawers without blinking.

Then she rustled across the room to my dresser. Again, she began to slide the drawers open, silently, one at a time.

I realized this was a dream when I saw her black shoes lift off from the floor. She floated halfway to the ceiling, and her arms became wings, long black feathery wings that flapped slowly, keeping her in the air.

In the dream, I felt relieved. I knew I was dreaming. I knew she hadn't really returned. It was a weird nightmare, but I no longer felt afraid.

I watched her turn into a large crow, floating easily to the ceiling. Then she tossed back her head, her long beak glowing in the blue light. She opened her beak and let out a terrifying sound — a squawk and a laugh. A shrill bird cackle that made the hairs on the back of my neck stand up and froze me in place. Even in the dream, the sound was so chilling, I couldn't move.

Then she closed the beak and turned her feathery head. She returned to the floor, landing softly, silently. Her wings turned back to arms. I could see her head shrink back to a human head, her hair down to her shoulders.

She turned and moved to my closet. In the dream, I knew what would happen next. I knew she'd go into the closet and find the mask I had stolen.

And what would she do next?

I didn't want to find out. I forced myself out of the dream.

Wake up, Scott. Wake up.

I sat up, blinking. Alert. The nightmare lingered in my mind.

I gazed around the room. No one there. No old woman. No giant black bird.

The morning sun, still red and low in the sky, washed in through my window. I stretched my arms above my head.

"Just a dream," I murmured. "Just a weird, frightening nightmare."

I took a deep breath.

"Hey!" I let out a cry.

And stared at the black feather on the blanket at the foot of my bed.

26

Saturday morning was a gray, cold day with swirling winds and dark clouds hanging low overhead. The perfect day to meet at the abandoned house across the street from the graveyard.

Amanda was waiting for me at the bottom of the front stoop, her parka hood up, her hands buried deep in the pockets. Her smile faded when she saw Rita tagging along with me.

"Rita is going to help us," I said. "She promised me she'd cooperate and not try to scare us all the time and not be a pest."

"That's *three* promises," Rita said. "I don't remember making three promises."

I scowled at her. "Do you want to help Amanda and me scare those three bullies, or not?"

A devilish smile crossed my sister's face. "Will you buy me a huge box of YORK Peppermint Patties?"

Amanda laughed. "She wants a bribe."

"Only kidding," Rita said. "Don't you two know when I'm joking?"

"This is serious," Amanda told her. "We are about to enter a major horror-movie world. We don't have time for jokes."

Rita glanced from Amanda to me. "You two are weird," she said. She raised her right hand. "I promise I'll be good."

A blast of wind made me shiver. It seemed to cut right through my coat. Across the street in the graveyard, crows began to *caw* in the branches of the bare trees. The sounds were raw and shrill, as if the big black birds were crying out to us, warning us away.

I shivered again. The crows reminded me of my nightmare the night before. "Let's go in," I said. I took a deep breath and led the way around to the side of the house.

We had trouble pushing the kitchen window open. I struggled and strained and nearly toppled backward off the window ledge. Finally, the frame creaked, and I managed to shove it up high enough. All three of us carried big bags of supplies. We had to drop the bags into the house, then slide in after them.

Breathing hard, I took a moment to look around. Everything seemed just as we'd left it. A layer of dust covered everything. The light from outside barely seeped through the dirt-smeared windows.

We didn't move. We listened hard. Silence. No wails or moans, no groans or creaks or squeaks.

"This place is gross," Rita said, rubbing her fingers through the dust on the kitchen table. "Are you sure you want to have your party here?"

"It will be the scariest Halloween party ever," I said.

And that was the plan.

To invite Mickey, Morty, and Kenji to the scariest Halloween party ever. In this dusty, creaky, smelly, rotting haunted house. And to make sure we terrified them out of their *skins*, my plan was to fill the place with scare after scare.

We walked through the dining room. The chandelier above the long table was almost hidden by cobwebs. At the end of the table, I could still see the rectangle shape in the dust where the box I'd stolen had stood.

The floorboards creaked as we stepped into the big front room. Morning sunlight struggled to wash in through the big windows that looked out onto the street.

Rita dropped her shopping bags of supplies and started to do a crazy dance. "Hey, I'm dancing in a haunted house. Think any ghosts are watching?"

"STOP!" Amanda and I both screamed at once.

Amanda stopped in mid-dance.

I pointed. "There's a trapdoor right in front of

you," I said. "If you step on the floor there, the floor drops about six feet down."

"Cool," Rita said. "Can I try it?"

"No way," I told her. "Stay away from it. We're going to give our three guests a nice surprise on that trapdoor."

She stuck her tongue out at me and made a spitting noise.

"Is that the way you cooperate?" I said.

She grinned. "Yes."

Amanda frowned at Rita. "Scott, are you sure we need her?"

"She's going to be the biggest scare of all," I said. "Trust me. I have it all planned out."

The wind howled outside, a burst so strong it made the front windows rattle. Amanda jumped. "This house is so scary in the daytime," she said. "Can you imagine how scary it will be at night?"

"Let's get to work," I said. I bent down and started to pull things from the shopping bags. "First of all, these are spray cobwebs." I held up the two cans. "We spray this stuff everywhere. And the cool thing is, the cobwebs have little plastic dead flies and spiders attached to them."

"That's definitely cool," Rita said. She grabbed a can and sprayed cobwebs down the front of my coat.

I grabbed the can back and frowned at her. "Settle down, okay?"

I pulled out the large plastic bags of green slime. "We let this stuff ooze down the wall," I said.

"I get it," Amanda said. "Protoplasm, right? The stuff ghosts leave behind."

I nodded. "Yeah. We tell our three 'friends' how fresh it looks. That means ghosts were here very recently."

"I brought the laptop," Amanda said. She opened it. "Listen to this." She hit a few keys, and I heard low moans. Then a loud whispered voice: *"Help meeeee. Helllp meee. Please . . . help meeeee."*

I knew it was a recording of Amanda whispering, but it still gave me a chill.

"We'll put it under that old couch over there," I said, pointing. "That'll make them jump."

"They'll want to run home," Amanda said. "They'll want to get out of here as fast as they can."

"And I'll pretend we're locked in," I said. "I'll act all terrified and panicky and keep trying the doors, and tell them someone locked us in."

I unrolled a small carpet I'd brought. "I'm putting this over the trapdoor. They won't be able to see the floorboards. When they step on the rug, down they'll go."

Amanda pulled long, filmy ghost figures from her bag. They were posters, but the ghosts glowed, which made them look 3-D. "We can hang one of these in the dining room."

I lifted two jack-'o-lanterns from my bag. They were plastic, and when you pushed a button, they opened their mouths wide and started to laugh.

"The three jerks probably won't get really scared till you start the explosions," Rita said. She handed me my old iPod. I'd filled it with terrifying loud explosions and people screaming.

"When the explosions start, they'll run for the door," I said. "That's when I pretend that the door is locked and we're all trapped inside."

Amanda shuddered. "It's good. I'm getting scared, myself."

"Is this when I do my thing?" Rita asked.

I nodded. "Yes. We've got the three guys in a panic, right? And then the final fright. Rita is all dressed in black — completely covered so no one can see her. She comes floating down the stairs wearing the evil death mask. All they can see is the mask floating on its own."

Amanda laughed. "That will terrify them forever!"

"They'll start crying like babies," I said. "After Halloween night, they'll be too embarrassed to bully us again."

The three of us all cheered and shook our fists above our heads. Then we went to work, setting up everything, putting all our scares in place. We had creepy things floating from the ceiling and oozing down the wall and popping out of doorways. We had eerie sound effects and moans and whispers and cries.

We had the laughing jack-'o-lanterns and the dripping protoplasm — and, of course, the terrifying explosions. It took us over three hours to get everything ready for the party.

"I'm starving," Rita said, as we gathered up the empty shopping bags. "It's way past lunchtime."

"Yes. Let's get out of here," Amanda said. "I've breathed in so much dust, I think I'm turning into a dust ball."

I folded the shopping bags under my arm and crossed the entryway to the front door. I grabbed the knob, twisted it, and pulled. The door didn't budge. I tried again. This time I pushed. I twisted the knob and leaned my shoulder into it.

No. Not moving.

I tried turning the knob the other way. Pulling. Then pushing.

My voice trembled as I turned to Amanda and Rita. "Hey, I don't believe it. We're locked in."

Rita laughed and shoved me away from the door. Amanda rolled her eyes. "Did you really think you could scare us, Scott? Did you really think we'd believe you?"

"We came in through the kitchen window, remember?" Rita said.

I shrugged. "Okay, okay. It was worth a try. I thought I'd give you a little fright."

"We had enough frights already this morning in this old house," Amanda said.

I led the way through the kitchen to the window. "I can't wait to get our three 'friends' in here," I said. "When we're finished with them . . ." My voice faded.

I stopped halfway across the room. All three of us stared.

"D-didn't we leave that window open?" I stammered.

"Yes, we did," Amanda said in a tiny voice.

"Well, it's closed now," I said. I strode over to it, raised my hands to the top of the frame, and shoved up as hard as I could. I tried again. Then I took a deep breath and pushed again.

A cold feeling of dread ran down my body. "Whoa," I murmured. "We really *are* locked in."

27

Again, Rita shoved me out of the way. "Are you joking? This isn't funny."

"I — I'm not joking," I said, my voice cracking. "Someone closed the window tight." I peered through the glass. No one out there.

"Okay. Let's not panic," Amanda said.

"Too late," I said. "I'm already panicking. Did someone *inside* this house shut the window on us?"

Before anyone could answer, I heard soft whispers from another room. At first, they sounded like a breath of wind. But as I stood there, frozen in fear, all of my senses totally alert, I began to make out a repeated word.

"*Stay . . . stay . . . stay . . .*"

I grasped Amanda's arm. "Do you hear that?"

Her eyes looked like they were about to pop out of her head. "Someone whispering?"

"I don't hear it," Rita said. "If you two are

trying to freak me out . . ." But then her mouth dropped open.

"*Stay. . . . You will stay . . .*"

"I hear it!" she cried. "Let's get out of here!"

Without saying another word, the three of us turned to the window. Working together, we gave a hard push and hoisted the heavy frame up. Then we dove out onto the side yard.

I landed on my hands and knees. Pain shot up and down my body, but I didn't care. I took off running along the side of the house to the street. Amanda and Rita were close behind me.

We turned left and started running toward home, our shoes pounding the sidewalk. When Mickey, Morty, and Kenji burst in front of us, we nearly knocked them over.

"Hey — whoa!" Mickey cried, raising both hands to stop us. "What's the big hurry?"

They wore tan sports jerseys with big red numbers on the front. All three of them had number 13. And they carried hockey sticks, which they waved in front of them.

"Just in time for the next meeting of the Dare Club," Morty said, grinning his ape grin. Kenji giggled, as if Morty had just said something hilarious.

"I didn't know you guys played hockey," I said.

"We don't," Mickey said. "We just think we look cool carrying hockey sticks." Kenji giggled again.

"You look like jerks," Rita said. She wasn't afraid of them. Even *they* wouldn't pick on a little girl.

Maybe.

We tried to edge past them, but they moved quickly to block our path. "Where are you going?" Morty asked. "Don't you want to hear your next dare?"

"We're late," I said. "I promised my mom I'd brush our dog's teeth this afternoon."

"You don't have a dog," Kenji said. "I know you don't have a dog."

"Hey, you're right," I said. "That's what I'm late for. I'm supposed to go to the pound and pick out a dog, and then brush its teeth."

Mickey turned to his twin. "Is this guy supposed to be funny?"

Morty shrugged. "Beats me."

"This is a simple dare," Mickey said. "We want you to sneak into that old house and stay in there for half an hour without scaring yourselves to death."

"Go in that old haunted house?" Rita said, pretending to be scared.

Amanda and I exchanged glances. The three bullies obviously hadn't seen us come diving out the window.

"Forget about that. We have a dare for *you*," I said.

Mickey sneered. "Don't make me laugh. I have chapped lips."

"Listen to our dare," Amanda said, arms crossed tightly in front of her parka.

"What are you doing for Halloween?" I asked. "Going over to the party at the elementary school to drink the little kids' blood?"

Morty turned to Mickey. "This guy is a riot."

"We have these awesome skeleton costumes," Kenji said. "We're going to hang by the grave- yard and give people a heart attack when they walk by."

"Good plan," I said. "But we have a dare for you. We dare you to come to *our* Halloween party."

They all got big sarcastic grins on their ugly faces. "Ooh, fun," Morty said. "Will we sing Halloween songs and carve our own jack-'o- lanterns?"

"Can we sit by the fireplace and tell ghost sto- ries?" Kenji asked.

They burst out laughing.

"It's not a baby party," Amanda said. "Our party is inside the old haunted house."

That stopped them. Their grins faded.

"Everyone knows that house is seriously haunted," Morty said.

I stuck out my jaw. "So?"

"So you're going to have a party in there?"

I nodded. "It's going to be the best Halloween party ever. And we *dare* you to come."

They grew silent. They exchanged glances. Then more silence.

Mickey burst out laughing. "I get it. Morty, Kenji, and I go into the haunted house. And you three never show up. Right?"

"Wrong," I said. "We'll be there."

"I don't like it," Kenji told the twins. "It sounds like a trap."

"We wouldn't trap you," I said. "We'd be too scared. After all, you dudes carry hockey sticks."

"We just want to have an awesome party," Amanda said. "And you're the only three guys we know who wouldn't be scared to go into that house on Halloween night."

I had to smile. Amanda really knew how to spread the flattery. I didn't think they could resist that.

And they couldn't.

"Okay. We'll be there," Mickey said.

"We accept your dare," his twin agreed. "But it better be a good party."

"Yeah, it better not be a baby party," Kenji said.

"Are you sure you three wimps won't be too terrified?" Mickey asked. "You'll be shaking and quaking and crying and begging us to let you go home."

"No, we won't," Rita answered.

"You're such total cowards," Mickey said, scowling at me. "I'll be surprised if you last ten minutes."

"Don't worry," I said. "There will be *plenty* of surprises for all of us."

And I was right.

PART FOUR

28

A huge storm hit our town Halloween morning. Big raindrops pattered my bedroom window and woke me up with a shock. I thought someone was pounding on the window.

Lightning crackled, and the thunder seemed to be right over our house. I walked to my window and gazed down to the street. A river of water rushed along the curb, and big gray puddles the size of ponds dotted the sidewalk.

Amanda and I were supposed to go to the old house to do a final check and make sure everything was ready for the party. But I had a stomachache. I'd raided the Halloween candy Mom bought for trick-or-treaters, and maybe I had too many Snickers bars.

Also, neither one of us felt like going out in the storm. We're both a little afraid of being hit by lightning. I told you, we're not the bravest people in the world.

But after the party tonight, we'd both have proof that we were braver than Mickey, Morty, and Kenji.

Amanda and I worked some more in the old house Wednesday and Thursday after school. We actually got the front door to open, which meant we all wouldn't have to climb in through the kitchen window.

We put the batteries in some eerie-looking, old-fashioned torches and hung them on the wall. We placed about a million candles everywhere.

We didn't hear any moans and groans. No whispers telling us to *stay*. That made us feel a little more confident.

We checked all of the scares we had planted, the jumping skeletons, the laughing jack-'o-lanterns, the filmy ghosts that were set to float down from the dark ceiling.

Amanda and I were excited. Everything worked perfectly. We knew we could terrorize the three bullies — especially when we told them we were locked in the house . . . trapped . . . and the ugly wooden mask came floating down the stairs on its own.

But then we had a disaster.

I was halfway up a ladder, trying to hang the big bag of green slime over the dining room door, and the bag broke. I screamed as the thick goo plopped onto my head, and I toppled backward off the ladder.

I landed hard on my back. I felt my breath whoosh out, and my chest throbbed. I struggled to breathe as the green goo oozed over my head, my face, my shoulders.

Amanda came rushing over and dropped down beside me on the floor. "Are you okay?"

"No," I groaned. "How am I supposed to breathe with this green gunk covering my nose and mouth?" That's what I *wanted* to say. But actually, it came out, "Glub glub glubbbb."

"You've ruined the ghostly protoplasm," Amanda said. "That was one of our best surprises."

"Glubbbb glub," I said. I tried to pull the disgusting stuff off my face with both hands. And now my hands were covered with it.

Amanda shook her head. "You'll never get it off."

"Thanks for your support," I said, finally pulling enough of it away so I could speak. "What if I go home and take a shower?"

"Probably won't help," she said. "The slime will stick to your skin."

I grabbed her hand and rubbed green gunk up and down both sides of it. Then I smeared some on her cheek.

She let out a shriek. And then we both started laughing. It was just so ridiculous.

After we stopped laughing, she helped pull me to my feet. Somehow I had stepped in the slime

137

and it was all over my shoes. It gave me an idea. I made slime footprints from the dining room door to the nearest wall. The footprints made it look as if some ghostly creature had walked to the wall and then just vanished.

"Very cool," Amanda agreed.

We went home happy, satisfied about our plan. I took a long, hot shower and most of the green slime washed off.

Now it was Halloween morning with thunder roaring right outside my window and rain beating against the glass like an ocean wave. The perfect weather to scare three bullies.

I helped myself to breakfast. Mom was at work. Rita was still asleep. She can sleep through anything.

My phone rang just as I finished my Corn Flakes. I squinted at the screen and saw that it was Mickey Klass calling. "Hey, Mickey. What's up?" I said.

"How's it going, Scotty?"

He knows I hate it when people call me Scotty. "Okay."

"Hey, listen. About your party," he said. "Morty and I and Kenji . . . we got a better invitation."

I made a gulping sound. "Huh? What did you say?"

"We changed our minds, Scotty. We're not coming to your party."

29

I squeezed my phone so hard, it popped out of my hand. It hit the rug and bounced a few times.

Not coming to the party?

I grabbed the phone in a trembling hand and raised it to my ear. "But — but — but —" I sputtered.

Mickey laughed, a nasty horse laugh. "Just messing with you, Scotty," he said.

"You mean —?"

"We'll be there. And you'd better be there, too."

My heart was still pounding. I let out a sigh of relief. *Even Mickey's jokes are cruel.*

"We'll be there," I said. "Eight o'clock."

"Sure that isn't past your bedtime?" He laughed his obnoxious laugh again.

You won't be laughing after tonight, Mickey, I thought.

*   *   *

Amanda, Rita, and I got to the old house at seven and started lighting candles. I have to admit I felt way tense. I mean, a lot was riding on this party. Like my whole life.

If it worked, Amanda and I wouldn't have to live in terror anymore. I could walk to school without having to worry about being heaved into an open grave. Life wouldn't be scary anymore. What a thrill that would be.

But as soon as we got all the candles lit around the abandoned house, we had a crisis. And, of course, the crisis was Rita.

"Why do I have to stay out of sight the whole time?" she demanded with her hands pressed against the waist of her solid black costume. "Why can't I enjoy the party, too?"

Amanda and I glared at her. "You're not *supposed* to enjoy the party," I said. "It's not that kind of party."

"It's not really a party," Amanda said. "It's just a way for us to terrify the three Neanderthals."

"You have to stay upstairs out of sight till the end," I said. "Then you come gliding down the stairs, all hidden in black, the death mask on your face, floating, floating down to scare them out of their heads."

Rita stamped her foot. "I get all that," she snarled. "But why can't I have pizza and soda and tortilla chips like everyone else?"

"We just explained," Amanda said.

"Why don't you take a slice of pizza *now*?" I said. "Take it upstairs with you."

"But I'm not hungry now!" Rita exclaimed.

A loud knock on the front door ended the argument. Rita grabbed a slice of pizza from the box on the food table and went running for the stairs.

I waited till she was totally out of sight and then pulled open the heavy wooden door. As promised, Mickey, Morty, and Kenji stood there in their skeleton costumes.

The costumes were actually awesome. If you like gross costumes. The skull masks had cracks across the foreheads and big painted spiders pouring from the cracks. The bones on the front of the costumes were yellowed and cracked. And smears of dark blood covered their chests. One of the costumes had a huge gray rat clinging to the bony ribs.

I stood to the side so they could enter the house. "Who are you supposed to be?" Kenji asked. "Wonder Woman?"

All three of them burst out laughing.

"No. Captain America," I said. I pointed across the room. "Amanda is a Martian princess."

"Did your mommy make that costume for you?" Mickey asked her. He flipped his fingers at one of the tall antennae on her head. She didn't answer him.

The three of them clomped across the front room, their skulls glowing in the candlelight.

They strode to the food table, and they each picked up big, two-liter bottles of Coke. The Coke was supposed to be for everyone. But they each tilted a whole bottle to their mouths and chugged.

Then they burped as long and loud as they could.

That made them laugh like fools, slapping each other high fives and bumping knuckles.

What jerks.

I tried to get down to business. "This house is definitely haunted," I said in a low voice.

"Have you guys ever been in a haunted house before?" Amanda asked them.

Before they could answer, a high, shrill scream broke the silence. I turned to the stairway. Did it come from upstairs?

Another scream of horror, so high-pitched it rattled in my ears.

Yes. It was definitely from upstairs.

The three skeletons froze, exchanging glances.

I turned to Amanda. I didn't know what to do. "Is that *Rita* screaming like that?" I whispered.

30

"I . . . don't think it's real," Amanda said, but her eyes were wide with fright.

"Did we set up scream sound effects upstairs?" I whispered.

"I don't remember."

Mickey and Morty stepped to my sides and bumped me between them. "Look. We made a Scotty sandwich," Morty said. They bumped me again. "Why don't you go upstairs and see who's screaming?"

"Uh . . . it stopped," I said.

Kenji was at the food table. He had taken off his skull mask so he could jam his mouth full of tortilla chips.

"This is way boring," Mickey said, yawning. "You call this a party? It's more like a funeral."

"I've taken geography tests that were more exciting than this," his twin agreed.

"And you probably *flunked* them, too," Amanda said.

"Don't forget, we're in a haunted house," I said. "Can't you feel the vibrations? Can't you feel there's some other presence here, a *ghostly* presence?"

Morty burped really loud again.

"Look at *that*!" I cried. I pretended to be surprised as I pointed to the footsteps across the floor at the dining room entrance. The footprints I'd made by stepping in the green goo. "Those footprints go to the wall and stop."

"Who cares?" Kenji said, spitting chips from his mouth as he talked.

I started to say something about ghostly protoplasm. But I stopped as something dark came floating down over us.

Dark and filmy, slipping down from the ceiling. Ghostly shadows, maybe a dozen of them. The eerie see-through figures floated down over us. They were cold to the touch. They felt like raindrops on my skin. The shadows dissolved as they hit the floor.

"I-I don't like this," Morty stammered. He swung his fists and tried to bat the shadows away. But his fist sailed right through them.

"Is this some kind of trick?" Mickey demanded.

Amanda and I exchanged glances. We didn't say a word. But we knew what the other was thinking.

The screams upstairs . . . the ghostly shadows swirling down on us . . .

These aren't the scares we planted!

144

31

I heard a loud clattering at the front window. A clicking and bumping as if someone was trying to break in.

I lurched toward the front of the room, and in the flickering candlelight, I saw bony fingers on the other side of the glass. Tapping ... tapping ...

And then a human skull rose into view. I swallowed. Amanda screamed.

We gaped at the skeleton slapping at the window. "It ... it's not a costume!" I choked out.

Mickey, Morty, and Kenji didn't move. They stared at the tapping bones without moving a muscle. Were they frozen in fear?

"*Ooohhhhhhhhh.*"

A deafening moan, like a dying animal, rose up at my feet. I spun around, expecting to see some kind of creature on the floor. But there was nothing there.

The skeleton at the window had vanished into the blackness of the night. I backed away. My whole body shuddered.

This isn't right. This isn't what Amanda and I planned.

What is happening here?

"Hey, what's that smell?" Mickey sniffed the air, then pinched his fingers over his nose.

"Yuck." Kenji made a sour face. "It *reeks* in here."

I took a deep breath and almost puked. "It . . . it's like poison *gas*," I whispered.

The three bullies began choking and sputtering and coughing. Tears rolled down their faces. They leaned on each other, groaning and complaining.

How to describe the putrid odor? It's like if you took decaying meat and spoiled milk and rotten eggs and burning tires and mixed them all together into one heavy, steamy smell.

Holding my arm over my mouth and nose, I staggered across the room to Amanda. "I'm trying to hold my breath," she said. "But the smell . . . it's *inside* me!"

"We have to get Rita," I told her, tugging her arm. My stomach lurched. "We have to get Rita and get *out* of here."

"I don't understand," Amanda whispered.

"These aren't the scares we set up. Why is this happening?"

"There's only one explanation," I said. "The moans we heard ... the whispers. The house really *is* haunted. And whoever is haunting this place is out to *scare us to death!*"

32

Amanda started to the stairs to get Rita. But Morty moved quickly to block her path. "What's wrong?" he demanded. "Where are you going?"

"We . . . have to get out of here," Amanda stammered. She dodged to the right. But Morty wouldn't let her pass.

"Get out? Why?" Mickey demanded. "The party just got started."

I realized the smell had lifted. I started to breathe normally.

"That had to be the smell of the dead," I said. "Don't you see? We're not safe here. This party was a bad idea."

Kenji grinned. "Are you joking? I think it's an *awesome* party." He grabbed a slice of pizza, rolled it up, and jammed it into his mouth.

"Okay, okay. Let me be totally honest with you guys," I said. I was breathing hard. Sweat rolled down my forehead.

"You're too scared to stay?" Kenji asked.

"You want to go home to mommy and have your apple juice?" Mickey chimed in.

"Do you suck your thumb?" Morty asked. "Seriously. Do you?"

"Listen to me!" I cried. "We have good reason to be afraid. You don't understand. We all have to get out of this house. There's something evil in here, and it's out to get us."

"He's telling the truth," Amanda said. "We're not just being wimps."

"You look like wimps to me!" Mickey said. The two others snickered.

"We set up a bunch of scares," I told them. "Amanda and I . . . we've been working in here all week. We put ghosts in the closet and scream sound effects all around and laughing jack-'o-lanterns and all kinds of creepy stuff. Because we wanted to give you guys a good scare."

"But we didn't do the stuff that's happening," Amanda told them. "That horrible smell . . . the skeleton at the window . . . the shadowy ghosts floating down from the ceiling . . . Those weren't ours!"

Mickey tore off his skeleton mask and squinted at Amanda. "You didn't do that stuff?"

"No," I said. "That's what we're trying to tell you."

Morty tugged off his mask and tossed it onto the table. "You mean —?"

"I mean we have to get out of here fast," I said.

"The house has scares of its own. And I have a very bad feeling the scares are going to get a lot worse!"

"So can we stop wasting time and *go*?" Amanda pleaded.

To my surprise, all three guys burst out laughing. They laughed and bumped knuckles and dropped onto their knees, laughing so hard they couldn't stand up.

Amanda and I stared at each other. My heart was pounding. I knew we were in horrible danger. What could be so funny?

"You fraidycats are too easy," Mickey said finally. "You're no fun. You're just too easy to scare."

I made a gulping sound. "Huh?"

"What are you saying?" Amanda said.

"WE planted those scares," Mickey replied. "We set them all up. We took yours out and put our scares in."

"We saw you sneak into this house last Saturday," Kenji said. "When you invited us to your party, we figured out what you were planning to do."

"It's not like we're idiots," Morty said. "It wasn't too hard to figure out. So we decided to make our own scares and see if we could teach you a lesson."

"But it's too easy to scare you," Mickey said. "It's no fun at all."

Whoa. Double whoa.

Have I ever been so angry and so upset and so frustrated in my whole life?

I don't think so.

Our big chance to take our revenge on the three bullies. *And they win again!*

How sad is that?

I let out a long sigh. "Guess you got us," I muttered.

"I was scared. I admit it," Amanda said, her eyes cast down at the floor.

"Might as well have some pizza before it gets cold," I said. I was halfway across the room to the food table when I saw something move at the stairway. "Hey —" I started to utter a cry, but it stuck in my throat.

Near the top of the stairs, I saw the ugly death mask. It looked even more grotesque in the flickering light of the candles. The mask floated in the darkness and began to move down, hovering a foot or so above the banister.

"Whoa. Look." I pointed.

We all turned and watched the mask float down the stairs, blue-orange in the shadowy light. Rita was hidden in her black outfit. You couldn't see her at all.

Mickey's mouth dropped open. Morty made a gurgling sound. Kenji's eyes widened in fear.

The mask appeared to bob in the air, all by itself. Slowly, silently, it descended the stairs.

Morty gurgled again. Mickey stood frozen, gaping at the frightening scene.

Finally! I thought. Finally, we scared these guys. Thank you, Rita. *Wouldn't you know it would be Rita to scare the pants off them!*

The mask hovered at the bottom of the stairs. Its ugly scowl even made *me* shiver.

I watched the three bullies, gripped in fright. Then, to my shock, Mickey darted forward. He trotted across the room, his eyes on the mask. "Who's wearing that mask?" he cried. "Who's there? Let's see who it is."

He didn't hesitate. He ran up to the mask — grasped it in both hands — and *ripped* it away.

Then we all screamed when we saw there was *no one* wearing the mask.

No Rita. No one. No one.

The ugly death mask was floating on its own.

33

"That's impossible!" I cried. I stumbled back, trying to get away from the floating mask.

All five of us stepped back. No one spoke. I couldn't take my eyes off the ugly, scowling mask.

Rita, where are you? Where?

And then laughter, cold, cruel laughter rang out from the mask. A woman's deep laugh, raspy and harsh.

Before the laughter ended, Mickey opened his mouth in a frightened scream. He turned, dropped his skull mask, and bolted toward the front door. We all followed him, our shoes clumping heavily on the wooden floorboards.

Another peal of laughter rang in our ears. It followed us to the front of the house.

Before we reached the front door, a thick swirl of purple mist rose in front of us. The mist spun crazily, spreading out, filling the dark room with an eerie purple light.

"Open the door!" Morty shouted to his brother. "Hurry — open it!"

We all stopped short as the purple mist parted, and a woman stood in front of us. She wore a long black dress down to the floor. I recognized her at once. Recognized her straight white hair, her pale skin pulled tight against her face, the gold tooth in the middle of her mouth as she smiled at us.

"Calm down, everyone," she said. "Take a breath. You're not going anywhere."

"Is that the woman you saw in your house?" Amanda whispered.

I nodded. I turned to the woman. "Who are you?" I cried in a trembling voice. "I know you're not my aunt Ida."

"Of course I'm not your aunt Ida," the woman said with a cold sneer. "Your aunt Ida is still *alive*, isn't she?"

Amanda gasped. Behind me, Mickey, Morty, and Kenji muttered to each other.

"Then who are you?" I demanded. "What were you doing in my house?"

"My name is Lillian," she said. "That's a lovely name, isn't it?"

"I guess," I said. I didn't know how to answer her.

"I used to be a lovely person," she said, her raspy voice a low whisper now.

"Are you going to answer my questions?" My voice broke. My legs were trembling. "Why were you in my room?"

"I was searching for the mask, of course," she snapped. "You came home from school before I could find it." She waved her hand in the air. The mask came floating across the room to her. She caught it and raised it toward us. "Thank you for bringing it back to me tonight. Your sister, Rita, and I have become very good friends."

Oh, no. Rita . . .

"Where is she?" I demanded. "Where is Rita? What have you done with her?"

Lillian waved a hand to calm me down. "Don't worry, Scott. You'll see your sister again. You'll have a lot of time to spend with her." She studied the mask as if seeing it for the first time. "I'm so happy to have this back. You did a bad thing — didn't you, Scott?"

All eyes were on me now. "Y-yes," I stammered. "I did. I'm really sorry I stole it. I don't know why I did it. It was crazy. It was wrong. I'm glad you have it back."

She smiled. Even in the dim light, the gold tooth gleamed. "I'm happy to have it back, too."

I took a deep breath. "So . . . we can all go home now?" I asked, my eyes on the door behind her.

She shook her head. "No," she whispered. "You won't be going home. You'll be staying here with me."

The words sent a shuddering chill down my back. "Forever?"

"Yes, Scott. Forever."

34

"You can't keep us here!" Mickey cried. He had his eyes on the door.

"I can do *anything*," Lillian replied. "I have the mask. I have powers you can't imagine." She narrowed her blue eyes at Mickey. "I can make you disappear."

"I'd *like* to disappear," Mickey said. "Right out that door."

"But I'm going to keep you here with me," Lillian said, spinning the mask on her pointer finger. "It's been so long since I had company."

"You . . . you've been living in this house?" I stammered.

She snickered. "I haven't been *living* anywhere. I've been trapped inside this mask for at least a hundred years. My spirit was trapped inside the mask, locked away in that wooden box." She squinted hard at me. "When you entered this house, you must have heard me wailing and moaning. So sad . . . so lonely."

"But — but —" I didn't know what to say.

She continued, her eyes locked on mine. "When you opened the box, I escaped from the mask. Escaped in a puff of purple mist."

I remembered the mist. Amanda and I were in my room. I opened the box, and the purple mist came shooting out.

"It felt so good to be free." Lillian shut her eyes. She seemed to be speaking to herself. "So good . . . so good."

"That means I *helped* you," I said. "I'm the one who set you free. So why can't you set *us* free?"

She flashed me a sad smile. Her gold tooth gleamed. "You don't know anything, *do* you? I *forced* you to help me. Didn't you feel my power pulling you to the box? I *made* you steal the box, Scott. I made you open it and release me. Did you really think you were in control?"

"I . . . I . . ." I sputtered.

Mickey edged up beside me. "She's an old woman," he whispered. "If we all rush the door at once, she won't be able to stop us."

"I don't think it's a good idea," I whispered back.

But Mickey didn't wait. He signaled with both hands, and he and Morty took off, racing for the door.

They didn't get two steps before they froze, then started to scream in pain. Their hands shot up to their ears. They wailed and slapped at their ears. I could see smoke floating up from their heads.

"Stop! Please stop it! Make it stop!" Mickey shrieked.

Lillian had one hand raised. She lowered it slowly.

"What did you *do* to them?" Amanda demanded.

Lillian offered a cold smile. "I set their ears on fire." She tossed back her head and laughed. "I turned their ears extra crispy!"

Mickey and Morty muttered to themselves, tenderly rubbing their blackened ears.

"I warned you," Lillian said softly. "I have all kinds of powers. You shouldn't think about escaping. You could get hurt."

"You're free now," I said. "And you have all your magical powers. So why do you need us? Why can't you let us go home?"

"Yes. Let us go home," Amanda echoed. "Please."

Lillian turned her eyes on me. "You don't understand, Scott," she said softly. "Let me explain the magic of the mask. In order for me to stay free, *someone else* must live inside the mask."

Amanda gasped. Morty made a choking sound.

Lillian had the mask in her hands and was moving toward me. Her eyes locked on mine.

She raised the mask, preparing to slide it over my face. "And I picked you, Scott. You've worn it before. You know it doesn't hurt."

"N-no!" I let out a stammered cry. I took a step back. Then another — and stumbled. "Ohhhh," I groaned as I tripped over Mickey's shoe. I landed hard on my back.

And before I could scramble to my feet, Lillian pushed the wooden mask over my face.

"You'll have such lovely dreams in there, Scott," she said. "You'll live in a wonderful fantasy world, forever and ever."

I tried to cry out, but the mask muffled my voice. She pressed the mask down hard. Harder.

I couldn't speak. I couldn't breathe.

I tried to kick and thrash and squirm out from under it. But Lillian had surprising strength. She smashed the mask against my face. . . .

Until I felt myself sinking into it. Falling into its darkness.

Once again, I saw the gray curtain of fog. And I heard the chattering voices, distant voices deep in the mask, rising and falling over a steady buzz of static.

I'm sinking, I realized. *Sinking into the fog, into the world of the mask . . . sinking so fast.*

35

I felt as if I was flying now, flying headfirst into a deep hole. Dropping faster and faster into the gray fog, into the chatter of strange voices. I knew I'd disappear and never return, never see the light again.

And just as I felt myself surrounded . . . lost in another world . . . at that very last moment, I heard a scream.

"Get off him! You can't do that to him!"

Was it Amanda? Amanda shouting from such a far distance?

Yes. Amanda's alarmed cry shook me awake. My mind fought off the gray fog. I clenched my jaw and opened my eyes and forced myself alert.

I grabbed the sides of the mask — and twisted my whole body to the side. I spun away from Lillian — and out of the powerful grasp of the mask.

I blinked myself alert. I breathed. My brain came back from the darkness.

Before I could move, Lillian came at me again with the mask raised. Her blue eyes burned with new intensity. She uttered a roar as she stabbed the mask back at my face.

"No way!" I screamed. I grabbed it from her hands and covered her face with it.

"Nooooooo!" Lillian's shriek of horror rang out as she stumbled into the mask.

She twisted and squirmed. But she was light and frail and no match for me. I kept it pressed tight against her.

"You can't do this!" she wailed. "You can't trap me in there again!"

But I pressed the mask over her. And as I struggled to keep it in place, she disappeared into it. First her head, her shoulders, her arms . . . pulled inside the mask by a powerful invisible force.

And then just before she sank completely into the mask, she let out a furious scream: "You can't keep me in here! You can't hold me! You can't! You *can't*!"

A loud burst — a deafening roar — made me let go of the mask and clap my hands over my ears. A sizzling puff of purple steam shot up from the mask, shot straight up to the ceiling. I watched the purple cloud float away and disappear upstairs.

The mask dropped from my hands and clattered to the floor. Lillian had vanished.

Morty, Mickey, and Kenji looked dazed. They stood there, blinking their eyes and shaking their heads.

Finally, Mickey spoke in a shaky voice. "Let's get out of here. You two sure know how to throw a party."

Morty gave me a shove. "Next time, have more pizza and fewer ghosts."

Our shoes thundered over the floor as the five of us stampeded to the front door. I tugged the door open, and we all ran out into the night. The cold air felt so good on my burning-hot face. I took several deep breaths.

I'm alive! I thought. *I'm not trapped inside a death mask forever.*

I turned to Amanda. "Do you want to come to my house?"

She shuddered. "I just want to get home."

I could understand that. I flashed her a thumbs-up and took off, running full speed.

I was halfway home when I remembered I'd forgotten something.

Rita. Rita was still back in the haunted house.

36

I spun around and hurried back to the house, my heart pounding. Of course, I didn't want to go back to that terrifying place. As I ran, my shoes felt as if they weighed a thousand pounds.

Rita. How could I forget Rita?

Rita was upstairs the whole time. Was she okay?

Clouds had floated over the moon, covering the street in darkness. I stopped on the sidewalk and stared up at the house. In our rush to escape, we had left the front door wide open.

I climbed to the top of the front stoop and cupped my hands around my mouth. "Rita? Are you in there?" My voice cracked as I shouted into the house.

I took a deep breath and stepped inside. The candles still flickered in the front room. I spotted the wooden death mask, facedown on the floor. My whole body shuddered at the sight of it.

I crossed to the stairs and shouted. "Rita? Are you still up there?"

Silence.

"Rita? Where are you? Are you upstairs?"

No answer.

I had no choice. I climbed the creaking stairs. I called her name again at the top. No answer. It was too dark to see anything up there. I slid my hand along the wall till I came to a doorway. "Rita? Hey, Rita? Answer me!"

My voice rang out down the hall. I moved slowly from room to room. No sign of Rita.

I returned to the stairs, a heavy feeling in the pit of my stomach. I called her name ten more times. Then, sick with dread, I slumped out of the house and walked slowly home. I'd never been so scared and worried in my life.

I left my sister upstairs in that house, and now she's gone.

I needed to tell Mom. I needed to get help.

I'll have to call the police.

The lights were on in the kitchen. I made my way to the kitchen door — and gasped in surprise. Rita sat at the kitchen counter, sifting through a pile of Halloween candy.

"Oh, wow! Oh, wow!" I exclaimed. "You're home! You're okay!" I was so happy and relieved, I ran over and *hugged* her!

She made a face. "Give me a break."

"How did you escape?" I cried. "How did you get out of that house?"

"I didn't escape," she said.

165

"Huh? What do you mean?" I cried.

"I didn't escape, Scott. I was upstairs. The purple mist came shooting upstairs. Remember? Lillian was inside the purple mist that shot out of the mask? It roared upstairs and settled over me."

"Settled over you?" My voice cracked. "Then what? What happened? What are you saying, Rita?"

She shrugged. "Never mind."

"No. Tell me. *Tell* me!" I demanded.

"No big deal," she said. She picked up a handful of candy. "Would you like a piece, Scott?"

She gave me a big smile.

A big smile . . . Yes, a big smile.

And I started to scream.

Because I saw the gleam of the gold tooth in the front of her mouth.

Goosebumps MOST WANTED

Who is pulling these strings?

NIGHT OF THE PUPPET PEOPLE

Here's a sneak peek!

"Jenny, don't fight with your brother. It's your birthday," Mrs. Renfro said.

"But he took the candy bar I wanted!" Jenny cried.

"Did not!" Ben squeezed the miniature Snickers bar in his fist. He made his mean face at Jenny.

Mrs. Renfro sighed. She blew a strand of blond hair off her forehead. "Why don't you two share it? You're twins. You should share *everything*."

"Ben never shares anything," Jenny pouted. She made a wild swipe for the candy in her brother's hand. But he snatched it away from her. "Get your own, Stink Head."

"Ben, don't call names on your birthday. You're five now. You have to act more like a gentleman."

"No, I don't," Ben insisted. "I don't even know what that means."

Mrs. Renfro had to laugh. She brushed a hand through Ben's curly brown hair. Ben was stubborn, but he knew how to make her laugh.

"Mom, don't laugh. He isn't funny," Jenny said.

Jenny loved scolding her mother. And she seldom let Ben bully her. Even though they were twins and looked alike, Jenny was already an inch taller than her brother.

Mrs. Renfro heard a shout and turned to the sound. All around the living room, the five-year-old party guests were smearing chocolate on their cheeks and chins. *I guess the little candy bars were a bad idea,* Mrs. Renfro thought. *I should have bought M&M'S.*

She pushed her way through the room. "What was the shouting about?" she asked.

Anna Richards, in a frilly pink party dress, pointed to the chubby boy with short black hair at the coffee table. "Jonathan spilled his apple juice," she reported. "He's a klutz."

Mrs. Renfro squinted at her. "Anna, where did you learn that word?"

"From *Sesame Street.*"

Jonathan Sparrow lived across the street. He and Ben and Jenny had playdates all the time. Now he was staring at a dark, wet spot on the front of his denim overalls.

"Don't worry about it," Mrs. Renfro said. "It'll dry."

"I spilled on the table, too," Jonathan said, avoiding her eyes.

She hurried to the kitchen to get paper towels. On her way back to the living room, the man with the long white beard stopped her. He wore a silky purple robe that came down to the floor. A tall, pointed red cap. And he had a long purple scarf wrapped around his neck.

"Is it time for the show?" he asked.

Mrs. Renfro nodded. "Good idea. Before it gets *really* messy in here!"

"Five-year-olds love chocolate," he said, scratching his beard.

She sighed. "I never should have given it to them." She waved the paper towels. "First, let me mop up a spill. Then we'll get started."

She hurried back to the living room. She glimpsed Jenny sitting cross-legged on the floor. Jenny had *three* candy bars in her lap. She always found a way to beat Ben.

Where was Ben? Wrestling on the rug with a red-haired boy from his kindergarten class.

"Let's all sit on the floor! Hurry!" she shouted. "Everyone sit down and face the fireplace. We have a surprise for you."

They were excited about the surprise, but it still took ten minutes to get them all seated. "Quiet, everyone!" Mrs. Renfro said. "Be very quiet. You don't want to miss the fun."

Ben and Jenny couldn't wait to find out what the surprise was. Mrs. Renfro smiled at their eager faces.

What a great idea it was to have this show, she thought.

Mrs. Renfro didn't know the horror was about to begin.

The man with the long white beard stepped quickly to the front of the room, swirling his long purple robe. "I am Wizzbang the Wizard!" he declared. His shout startled Ben, who bounced on the floor beside his sister.

"I have some magic to show you!" the wizard shouted. "Does anyone want to see some magic?"

The kids obediently cried yes.

Ben squinted at the wizard, who moved rapidly from side to side, his robe swishing over the rug. What was that in his long beard? A black spot that appeared to be moving.

Was that a spider in his beard?

Ben shivered. He didn't like spiders. Once, a spider got into his bed and crawled under his pajama shirt while he was just falling asleep. It didn't bite him, but Ben felt itchy every time he thought about spiders.

"Here comes the magic!" Wizzbang exclaimed. "Watch carefully, everyone."

Ben forced himself to look away from the black spot in the wizard's beard. He reached over Jenny and punched Jonathan on the shoulder.

"Shhh." Jonathan raised a finger to his lips. "I'm watching."

Wizzbang reached a hand under his robe and pulled out a tall marionette. She had a sparkly tiara on her head and was dressed in a long blue ball gown. It took Wizzbang a few seconds to get her strings untangled. They were attached to crisscrossed wooden control sticks. He sorted them out and made her stand up straight.

"This is the princess!" he announced. He leaned over the puppet. His long beard brushed the top of her tiara. Using both hands on the sticks, he made her take a few steps toward the audience.

"The princess is not a puppet. She is a mario-nette. But when Wizzbang the Wizard pulls her strings, she comes alive."

Ben stared at the princess as Wizzbang made her do a graceful dance. "She's almost as tall as we are," Jenny said.

"So what?" Ben replied. Jonathan laughed.

"Be quiet," Jenny snapped.

Ben watched the puppet dip and glide. Her eyes looked like real people eyes. Her lips were painted in a pale red smile. Beneath the tiara, her straight blond hair looked real, too.

Wizzbang pulled a string and made her raise one hand above her head. Then he moved the string, and her hand bobbed up and down as if she were waving to the kids.

"The princess has come from far away to wish happy birthday to Ben and Jenny," the wizard said. He made the marionette walk up to Ben. Her glassy eyes appeared to gaze down at him.

Ben raised himself to his knees. He took the puppet's small hand and pretended to shake hands with her.

Some kids laughed. But not for long.

The princess dipped suddenly. Her head dropped. Her mouth opened. And her wooden jaw clamped tight over Ben's shoulder.

He let out a cry of pain.

He tried to shake the puppet off. But her jaw tightened even harder, biting into his skin.

"It HURTS!" Ben screamed at Wizzbang. "Take her OFF me! It hurts. It REALLY hurts!"

Wizzbang's mouth dropped open. "I-I don't understand," he stammered.

He let go of the strings and wrapped both hands around the puppet's head. After a short struggle, he pulled the puppet off Ben.

"It . . . really . . . hurts . . ." Ben murmured. He was trying hard not to cry. He didn't want to cry on his birthday in front of all the kids. He rubbed his shoulder, but the pain kept shooting down his whole body.

"What happened?" Ben heard his mother ask. She was standing behind the kids, at the doorway to the dining room.

"The strings must have gotten tangled up," Wizzbang said. "And the mouth got stuck. Sorry, Ben." He rubbed Ben's shoulder. "Not to worry. I have another puppet."

He returned a few seconds later with a new puppet. This one had a crown on his head and wore a flashy leopard-skin robe.

"Say hello to the sultan," Wizzbang said. "He's the king."

Ben was still rubbing his shoulder. He heard a few kids talking about the puppet that bit him. They sounded scared.

"Ben, I'm sorry about the princess," the wizard said. "It was a bad accident. But you're okay, right?"

Ben nodded and muttered yes under his breath.

"These puppets are really fun to operate," Wizzbang said. "Would anyone like to stand up and work the sultan?"

No one raised a hand. The room grew very silent.

"It's very simple," Wizzbang said. "You pull the strings. Just like this." He made the sultan bow. Then he pulled some strings and the puppet's hands shot up in the air.

"Who would like to try it?" the wizard asked. "Jenny? You're the birthday girl. Come up here and meet the sultan."

Jenny climbed to her feet slowly. She glanced at Ben, then stepped up to the front of the room.

"Come closer," Wizzbang said. "Why are you standing so far away?"

Jenny frowned at the puppet. "Does he bite?"

About the Author

R.L. Stine's books are read all over the world. So far, his books have sold more than 300 million copies, making him one of the most popular children's authors in history. Besides Goosebumps, R.L. Stine has written the teen series Fear Street and the funny series Rotten School, as well as the Mostly Ghostly series, The Nightmare Room series, and the two-book thriller *Dangerous Girls*. R.L. Stine lives in New York with his wife, Jane, and Minnie, his King Charles spaniel. You can learn more about him at www.RLStine.com.

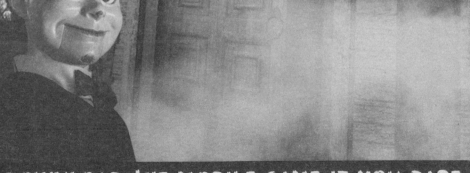

Goosebumps
THE GAME

Experience the thrills and chills of the Goosebumps Universe!

PLAY THROUGH A NEW AND ORIGINAL STORY

BATTLE OVER 20 CLASSIC GOOSEBUMPS CREATURES

EXPLORE THREE SPRAWLING, HAUNTING AREAS

FACE OFF AGAINST THE ULTIMATE CHALLENGER — SLAPPY THE DUMMY

IT IS COMING AND YOU CAN'T STOP IT!
FALL 2015

Available on Nintendo 3DS™, PC, Xboxlive Arcade, Playstation network, XboxOne and PS4

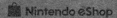

THE ORIGINAL Goosebumps BOOKS
WITH AN ALL-NEW LOOK!

R.L. Stine's Biography

REVENGE OF THE LIVING DUMMY
R.L. STINE

CREEP FROM THE DEEP
R.L. STINE

MONSTER BLOOD FOR BREAKFAST!
R.L. STINE

THE SCREAM OF THE HAUNTED MASK
R.L. STINE

DR. MANIAC VS. ROBBY SCHWARTZ
R.L. STINE

WHO'S YOUR MUMMY?
R.L. STINE

MY FRIENDS CALL ME MONSTER
R.L. STINE

SAY CHEESE - AND DIE SCREAMING!
R.L. STINE

WELCOME TO CAMP SLITHER
R.L. STINE

THE SCARIEST PLACE ON EARTH!

HALL OF HORRORS—HALL OF FAME
FOR THE TRULY TERRIFYING!

Catch the MOST WANTED Goosebumps® villains UNDEAD OR ALIVE!